"John Dally offers us a m̲ ̲ ̲ ̲ ̲ ̲ ̲ ̲ ̲ ̲ ̲ ̲ ̲ ̲ collection of stories full of heartbreak, faith, and lov̲ imagination and profound s̲ nothing less than the kaleidoscope of humanity in all its twists and turns, joys and sorrows, foibles and faithfulness."

MW01061490

— **The Rev. Tim Schenck, Rector of St. John the Evangelist Episcopal Church in Hingham, Massachusetts and @FatherTim on Twitter**

"We encounter the 'thin places' that join the worlds of Christian faith and gay life in these stories, rediscovering the workings of fate, circumstance, and mystery in the concrete particularities of everyday life. Dally brings a sensuous intelligence and historical imagination to his accounts of unexpected meetings and shared moments. The master is here, whether called or not, and he offers an 'accidental theology' for spiritual seekers and nonbelievers alike."

— **William Borden, University of Chicago**

"*The Master Is Here* is a literary tour de force. Sweden in 1842. West Virginia in 1937. Yale undergraduates in 1969 watching Dick Cavett interview men involved in the Stonewall Uprising. Partnerships are achieved or rejected or lost or mended as vividly distinctive characters navigate the universal hazards of the human condition: am I a good person, worthy of love and belonging? How do I cope with the variety of human relationships—love unsought or unrequited, people who are honest or abusive, desire that is confused or confusing? Woven through these universals, two distinctive threads: the reality of social disapproval and the power of Christianity as the West's dominant conceptual language for thinking about the human condition. For better for worse, Christianity matters—a reality Dally portrays in delicate, psychologically astute, theologically sophisticated ways. With exquisite literary skill, Dally brings each story to an adept, honest, solidly satisfying conclusion. The paradoxes and complexities of these lives remain intact, unsullied by cliché or platitude. Life may have no easy answers, but it sure has some terrific questions."

– Catherine M. Wallace PhD, cultural critic and author of *Confronting Religious Denial of Gay Marriage: Christian Humanism and the Moral Imagination*

"The characters in John Dally's *The Master is Here* are briefly sketched, yet fully drawn. A few, I wanted to throttle; many, I wanted to embrace. All left me intrigued and wanting to know them better, and that is a mark of beautifully crafted short stories. These glimpses into lives intersecting with gayness and Christianity are for everyone who cares about people and their experiences both unique and universal. They're for all of us who yearn for beauty, meaning, and connection in this life, and maybe even in a next one."

– Rhonda M. Lee, author of *Seek and You Will Find: Discovering a Practice of Prayer*

THE MASTER IS HERE

With many, many thanks for helping me get here.

THE MASTER IS HERE

STORIES CHRISTIAN AND GAY

JOHN ADDISON DALLY

TORTOISE BOOKS
CHICAGO, IL

CONTENTS

Introduction

Stories Christian and gay...is that a thing? The subtitle of this collection came to me without reflection and immediately felt exactly right, but I wasn't sure whether "Christian and gay" was an established category of some kind, so I Googled it. Top hits included the Metropolitan Community Church (good for them), support groups for Christians struggling to come out, and individuals named Christian Gay (they had my sympathy).

In our polarized country these labels might almost be considered mutually exclusive, especially since the backlash to marriage equality has chosen to employ the strategy of "religious freedom" to reestablish discrimination. That's why this collection is all the more timely. It does not proselytize for either the Christian faith or the gay community; the stories simply take place at the intersection of the two. Sometimes the characters are active, believing Christians, and sometimes they simply move about in the ruins of Christian empire. But one thing is consistent: their gayness is neither problematized nor valorized; it is just the window through which they look out at the world. Some of the characters are very good people, a few very bad people, but most simply find themselves in situations dire or ridiculous and have to figure out what they're going to do next.

In the early 1980s I was Artist-in-Residence at Saint Peter's Lutheran Church in New York City, shortly after the iconic slope-roofed Citicorp Tower had been built on the former church's footprint at 54th and Lexington and a new sanctuary incorporated into the skyscraper's ground floor. I learned of a conference to be held at the church for Christian artists and eagerly signed up. When the day of the conference arrived, I was handed a name badge that said "Hi! My Name Is _____and I'm Claiming the World for Christ Through_____" (fill in your artistic medium). I stared at the badge for a moment before putting it back on the table and heading out the door. I suspected I would not get much out of the conference, and that my gayness would most likely not be welcome. To be fair, I didn't give the organizers of the event a chance to prove me wrong, but anyone who was born in the 1950s (as I was) and grew up gay in America has learned to scent the wind pretty accurately and know when our emotional or physical safety is at risk.

I was raised in an atheist household but wanted to be a Christian from the time I could watch Mass for Shut-Ins on TV. (I was under the impression it was a cooking show.) My eventual confirmation in the Episcopal Church as a teenager and later ordination as a priest was not a rebellion against my upbringing, which still informs my way of being in the world and makes me cringe at some of the flights of fancy some Christians, ordained and lay, call theology. In fact, my non-religious upbringing freed me from the baggage so many LGBTQ folk have had imposed on them in the name of God.

From my earliest recollections I was both Christian and gay, with no struggle involved, and in writing these stories I wanted to share that perspective with a wider audience in the hope that it might encourage, confirm, and by all means entertain.

The Master is Here

Number 40 *Oudezijds Voorburgwal* looks pretty much like every other seventeenth-century townhouse I've seen in Amsterdam: tall and narrow, topped by a stair-step gable made of the same red brick as its walls. I'm damn near risking my life to get here, clinging to a tiny strip of sidewalk between the canal and a cobbled street where compact cars whizz by too close for comfort. But Renée said I had to see this place, so here I am, smack in the middle of *De Wallen*, the city's red light district. (A detail she omitted...so like her.) A discreet plaque identifies the house as *Ons' Lieve Heer op Solder*—Our Dear Lord in the Attic.

I press down hard on the thumb latch and hear the bolt jerk up on the other side of the door—no updates on the hardware—and pass into the low-ceilinged entrance hall. The musky scent of old wood is overpowering.

"*Middag*," says a sixty-something man in a cardigan standing behind a glass display case.

"Hello," I reply, outing myself as a non-Dutch speaker.

The man behind the counter switches easily to English. "Have you come to see the museum?"

"Yes."

"It's an hour till the next guided tour, but you're welcome to take this *boak*" (a slight slip in his otherwise flawless accent) "and see the place for yourself. We have an audioguide as well. Eight euros for the entrance fee and guidebook, twelve with the audioguide."

"Thanks, I'll just take the book."

I hand him my money and he surprises me by ringing up the sale on a cash register, an anomaly in this country where everyone pays for everything with their phones.

"Is the machine original to the house?" I ask.

He smiles weakly as he hands me my change. He's heard that one before. "Enjoy your tour."

"*Bedankt*," I reply. Single-word answers are manageable.

I start reading as I climb the stairs to the first floor: *Built as a gathering place for Roman Catholics prohibited from worshiping publicly after The Alteration of 1578, Our Dear Lord in the Attic was both a church and a home for the Catholic community's resident priest.*

At the top of the first set of stairs I come to a room the guidebook identifies as the *sael*—salon—handsomely furnished in Flemish Baroque style. High-backed chairs surround a massive oak table, and a two-tiered brass chandelier hangs from the deeply coffered wood ceiling. The floor above that contains the priest's study and bedroom, also beautifully restored with small details that make it seem as though the occupant has just stepped out of the room. At the top of the house (I already know from Renée) is the chapel that gives the museum its name. I expect something modest, like the closet chantries of recusant English manor houses, a space that could easily be disguised in times of duress. Yet when I emerge from the narrow stairway I find myself in a grand Counter-Reformation church, two stories high and looking very permanent indeed. A floor has been removed to create this soaring space, and two U-shaped balconies, one suspended above the other, wrap three of the four walls to provide additional seating. Only the treetops fluttering outside the clear glass windows remind me I'm on the top floor of a city house.

I sit down in one of the chairs lined up like pews in front of the altar. Dappled May sunlight filters through the elm leaves and traces changing patterns on the ancient wood of the floor, deepening the silence. At the altar, marble columns support a canopy surmounted by trumpet-blowing cherubs and frame an immense oil painting of the baptism of Christ. Embroidered in large letters across the front of the rich brocade frontal are these words:

MAGISTER ADEST ET VOCAT TE

I recognize the quote from the Gospel of John, but it confuses me. "The master is here, and calls you." Altar frontals don't typically have texts on them, but when they do it's usually something like *Holy, Holy, Holy* or *Behold the Lamb of God.* Why this snatch of dialogue from the story of Martha and Mary, the moment when Martha goes to call her sister to

Jesus? I look around the grand room, trying to imagine myself a prohibited Catholic in the Amsterdam of the late 1600s. What would the words mean to me? Some reference to the imminent raising of Lazarus, Mary and Martha's deceased brother? "Our community will rise again?" No, that feels like a stretch. Maybe something like "Come to the master, here at the altar?" That seems better. Then it comes to me all at once. "The Master is *here*," the frontal is telling the congregation, truly present in the eucharistic bread. The Mass is no mere memorial, as the Calvinist reformers of Holland insist, but a living encounter with the Son of God, who "*calls you*" to be faithful to this belief in a time of trial. The hair on my neck tingles as the centuries between me and that vanished congregation collapse.

I continue my tour through a curtained doorway to the left of the altar. In the rooms off the back stairway (originally an adjoining house) tall glass cases display a variety of devotional objects: altar crosses, pyxes, reliquaries, and, most strikingly, monstrances—elaborate metal stands for the exhibition of the consecrated Host. The Dutch diamond trade was at its height when this house church was built, and one solid gold monstrance from the community's treasury boasts two sparkling rows of them around the glass container at the center of its gaudy sunburst. I've never seen anything like it.

On the ground floor I return the guidebook to the ticket seller and head back out into the cool spring afternoon.

Continuing south on *Oudezijds Voorburgwal*, I turn right into *Oudekerksplein*. *De Wallen* begins to live up to its reputation as I pass window after window with young women offered for sale like meat in a butcher's shop or pies at the bakery. They remind me of the monstrances I just saw, sitting in their glass display cases like the Host, even offering the same invitation—Look at my body!—but no diamonds adorn their presence. Some of them strike alluring poses; others stare blankly; one reads a magazine.

The street opens out into Old Church Square, and there, standing brazenly in front of the looming bulk of the *Oude Kerk* itself, is Els Rijerse's *Belle*, a bronze sculpture of a prostitute standing proudly in a doorway. *Respect sex workers all over the world*, reads the inscription.

I continue following *Oudekerksplein* out the other side of the square and pass more of the windows. At the rear of one of the enclosed rooms a curtain parts and a young woman sticks her head in to say something to her colleague. In the dim room behind her the outlines of their pimp can just be made out, pacing impatiently. MAGISTER ADEST ET VOCAT TE, she seems to be saying, like Martha to Mary: the master is here, and calls you. The young woman nods and gets up from her chair, which her colleague then assumes.

I walk into a sleek little coffee bar and order an espresso and a shortbread cookie I've become inordinately fond of called a *zand gebak*. While I stand waiting at the counter I pull out my cell to call Renée back in The Hague and tell her about my visit to Our Dear Lord in the Attic. As her line begins to ring my eye wanders aimlessly, taking in the view out the open sliding doors. A slender blond teenager in a black leather jacket is leaning in the doorway of the newsstand across the street, watching me purposefully. He snaps to attention the moment our eyes meet and darts across the street to the coffee shop, ready to reel me in. Up close he's almost as tall as I am but he can't be more than fifteen. I think: Idiot! You're in the *Rosse Buurt*. Looking directly at anyone is like holding up a paddle at an auction.

Renée's voice mail kicks in and I have to decide whether to hang up or act as though she's answered live. If I hang up I'll have to deal with the young man, but if I pretend I'm absorbed in conversation the whole thing will get recorded on her voice mail. I take the coward's way out and begin a fake but lively exchange, trying to ignore the boy in the leather jacket. He leans one elbow on the counter and runs his other hand through his heavy bang. The tiny smile at the corner of his mouth lets me know he is willing to be patient. I turn my back on him, thinking of how I'll explain the situation to Renée later and hoping he'll get the message that I'm not interested. I'm disappointed in this. When I turn again he's still there, looking at me soulfully, mouthing the words "Thirty euros." Why isn't this kid in school where he belongs?

The barista puts my coffee and cookie on the counter and slides the *rekening* under the saucer. I realize I've fallen into a Graham Greene novel with no good exit strategy. I want to lecture this young man, berate him for having sex with people he doesn't know for money, plead with him to have more self-respect, to consider his family, his health, but I know perfectly well a talk like that will probably just yield me a shrug before he goes looking for a more willing trick.

As I continue my conversation with Renée's voicemail I note that the young man is wearing a clean white button-down shirt, khakis, and new loafers; he's no street urchin. Maybe he comes to *De Wallen* to earn drug money; maybe he's just doing it for a lark, to spite his burgher parents. I have no intention of figuring it out. I slap a five-euro note down on the bar for the coffee and hand him forty more, scowling to express my disapproval before turning and fleeing the coffee shop.

Masterful.

I walk quickly up the street but he's right behind me.

"Hey!" he calls out peremptorily. He sounds offended, maybe even a little hurt.

"Hey" is the same in English and Dutch, so I'm still not clear about his nationality.

"What's the big idea?" His English is idiomatic but Dutch-accented. I have no choice but to turn and face him. "I'm not a beggar," he says, looking at me defiantly. "If you're not interested just say so."

He waves my forty euros in front of me and I take it back meekly. "Sorry."

I stuff the money into my wallet and stare at my shoes, waiting for him to leave, but he doesn't. I sense that he's waiting for me to look at him, so I obey.

"*Wat een amateur,*" he says, holding my gaze, and I don't require a phrase book to take his meaning. "*Ik dacht dat je leek interessanter dan dat.*"

He's lost me now, but I gather it's not complimentary. I'm a little confused about why we're even having this conversation. He could have made an easy forty euros and moved on. What does he want?

"*Je toeristen komen naar De Wallen...*"

The dressing down continues, one sarcastic sentence after another, until I decide I've really had enough.

"OK, I get it. I think. I just didn't know the rules."

He seems taken aback by this. He cocks his head to one side and looks at me, considering. Then a broad smile spreads across his face.

"You never drank your coffee," he says. "You should go back. You can buy me one, too."

We return to the coffee bar and find my espresso still sitting there, the *gebak* and five-euro note untouched. He plunks himself down on a stool and swings his legs toward the counter, dropping a canvas rucksack on the floor at his feet. I take the seat next to him. The barista is drying glasses at the other end of the bar. The young man places his thumb and forefinger on either side of my cup appraisingly.

"*Dit is niet langer warm genoeg.*" He lifts his chin toward the barista, who notices the gesture immediately.

"*Twee koffie, alstublieft.*"

The barista nods and moves down to where we're sitting. He takes my undrunk espresso away impassively, as though customers ordering coffee and then disappearing only to return moments later with handsome underage strangers were a regular occurrence. In this part of town, maybe it is.

As the coffee machine hisses twice in succession the young man takes my shortbread and breaks it neatly in two, placing each half on napkins he's taken from a dispenser. He slides one of the halves over to his part of the counter.

"*Je wilt niet dik worden*," he says, by way of explanation. "You don't want to get fat."

I instinctively straighten up and suck my gut in. I'm not fat—at all—but when someone half my age raises the specter I have to reassure myself. He notices.

"Don't worry, you're fine."

He smiles to himself, clearly finding me all too easy to manipulate. I begin thinking of ways to redeem myself and intrigue him, at the same time wondering why I'm making such a plan. What if he's jail bait in the employ of the Amsterdam police? Do they have laws against entrapment? I don't want to find out.

"Look, um..." I need a name to complete my sentence.

"Thijs."

Thijs, like rice with a "t," short for Matthijs, Matthew.

He turns and offers his hand to me in a thoroughly American way, his face as free of guile as a Midwestern farm boy's. I shake it and find his grip surprisingly strong. Maybe I'm wrong about his age. He swivels back to the counter and picks up his cup.

"I'm Michael. Look, Thijs, I just don't do this kind of thing..."

"What kind of thing?" he asks, taking a sip of his coffee and contemplating his reflection in the mirror behind the bar.

"Um, you know, have *encounters* with people who are, you know, not quite...."

He pulls a wallet from his inside his jacket, takes out his driver's license and hands it to me. I look into his increasingly familiar face and hope that when I look down at the ID it's going to give me a big gift. It does. He's nineteen.

I smile sheepishly and slide the license back to him across the counter.

"Thanks. You could pass for fifteen until you open your mouth. I just wouldn't want to..."

"Go to jail?"

Geez, this kid doesn't pull any punches. "Well, that, of course, but I'd also be concerned for you..."

He snorts. "I'd be more concerned about yourself, if I were you."

He's probably right. I'm already falling for him.

"I'm a priest, you see."

He slams his cup down onto the saucer, making the barista wheel around to see what happened. "A *priest*? A *Catholic* priest?" He looks horrified. One of his feet slips to the floor, as though he might dismount and flee.

"Well, not exactly. An Episcopal priest...Church of England, you know?"

His face relaxes again and he pulls his foot back onto the chair rail.

"Ah, *Anglicaans*. Better. No one here goes to church, but we read about you in the news. The gays, the women, it's all good."

"Um, thank you, I guess."

"So what brings you to my city, *mijnheer pastoor?*"

"I'm doing some research. I'm interested in the relationship between religion and sexuality. I'm working on a book."

He turns his head slightly toward me, looking at me almost suspiciously out of the corner of his eye.

"I, too, am interested in that relationship."

Really? A fifteen—er, nineteen-year-old? Is he pulling my leg? "I thought no one here went to church. I assumed that included you."

"One does not need to go to church to think about religion. It is everywhere in Europe, crumbling into ruins. Of course, now that *Slotervaart* is full of burqas our Christian chauvinism has reawakened. The Muslims makes us think of God when we would rather forget him."

Could this guy really be nineteen? Nineteen going on fifty, and a well-informed fifty at that. Why the hell is he in the *Rosse Buurt* offering himself for thirty euros? The longer I listen to him the more confused I become, but I feel too shy to ask for explanations. I decide to give being intriguing another try. "I visited the museum of *Ons' Lieve Heer op Solder* this afternoon...you know it?"

"Of course."

"I saw a monstrance—do you know the word?"

He pulls out his phone and Googles it. After a few taps he turns the screen toward me and shows me a Wikipedia picture.

"*Ja, monstrans*, it's the same in Dutch."

"It was made of beautifully worked gold, and it had a double row of diamonds around the container for the Host."

Thijs' eyes widen.

"I was thinking about it when I left the museum and walked here and saw all the women in their windows..."

"*Ja, de raamprostituees...*"

"I thought how they were just like Jesus in his glass container, their bodies on display, but no one was going to call them holy, or surround them with diamonds. And I wondered how we got to the place where we say Jesus's body is holy and worship it, but we despise other bodies because they remind us of sex. I mean, Jesus was a great *friend* of prostitutes, wasn't he?" I'm a little surprised by my own vehemence. "I'm sorry. That's the kind of thing I think about it. Bored yet?"

"I like what you have said. Show me."

"What?"

He picks a cookie crumb from his lower lip and looks at it meditatively before tossing it away.

"Show me the *monstrans*."

I have an appointment to visit the *Stadsarchief* to look at some seventeenth-century journals from members of the English court in exile, but spending time with Thijs seems a lot more interesting, so we finish our coffee and retrace my steps to the museum. The young woman who had been summoned from the window by her pimp is standing now in the middle of *Oudekerksplein*, arguing with him loudly. I don't recognize the language they're speaking.

Thijs seems to read my mind. "There are a lot more Bulgarian women these days. She probably wants to know when the hotel maid job she was promised is going to materialize. They were all promised something to get them here, you know. No one wakes up one morning and says 'I think I'll move to Amsterdam and become a *raamprostituee.*'"

As we pass the statue of *Belle* Thijs waves a hand dismissively at it.

"*Wat een grap.*"

"What?"

"What a joke. Look at her...she's Dutch. Did you see any Dutch women in the windows you walked by? *Nee.* They are African, Caribbean, Asian. If you see a European she's probably Hungarian or Macedonian. The Dutch prostitutes are done with being a tourist attraction; they're in the clubs, or they have websites. These women didn't choose to be here; they were tricked or drugged or kidnapped and now they can't go home and they can't find another way to live. All so the guidebooks don't have to be rewritten."

Thijs' bitterness cows me. It also confuses me. How does his offer of himself for thirty euros relate to his tirade? Did someone drug or kidnap him? But no, this is his home. His clothes are first-rate; is he someone's kept lover? But then why

25

go sell himself in De Wallen? It occurs to me that if I'd just said OK when he said thirty euros I'd already know. Maybe I never will, now. We walk along in silence.

On the far side of the square Thijs hesitates, unsure of the museum's location. I indicate a left turn into *Oudezijds Voorburgwal* and he nods. For the second time today I open the stiff latch at No. 40 and go into the aromatic lobby. The man in the cardigan is still there. A few tourists are browsing the book display. The man raises his eyebrows when he sees that I've returned. When he notices Thijs at my side, they go higher. Does he recognize him? I glance at Thijs to see whether it's mutual but he's looking randomly around the room, uninterested in the docent.

"I'm back."

"Yes?"

"I believe I left my glasses somewhere inside. May I go and look?"

The request sounds perfectly reasonable to me, but he's not buying it.

"Will *he* be joining you?"

Thijs becomes alert when he realizes that he's being discussed.

"Uh, yes."

The man in the cardigan seems unhappy about the situation, though I have no idea why.

"Look, why don't I just pay you for two admissions?"

"I think that would be best. One adult and one child. Twelve euros, please."

"Two adults."

I hand him sixteen euros and the cash register rings once more. Thijs looks at the machine quizzically. We walk past the docent to the stairs.

"Good luck finding your glasses," he calls after us.

We come to the second floor *sael* just as the last visitor leaves it for the next floor.

"What was that guy's problem?" I say aloud, not expecting an answer.

"*De winkelbediende?*"

"Um, OK."

"It means...'shop clerk.' I can tell you."

"Really?"

"Yeah. I didn't recognize him at first. He hit on me last week on the *Warmoesstraat* and I turned him down. Guess he still has a...I don't know that word. *Een wrok.*"

"I'm guessing a grudge."

"*Grudge?* That's actually a word in English?"

"Yes."

He laughs. "It's stupid."

I find the entire Dutch language stupid, but decide to let it pass. Thijs has no interest in anything but the monstrance so we climb directly to the church and I lead him toward the room at the back where the liturgical vessels are displayed. At the doorway I realize I've lost him. I turn and see him planted in front of the altar, his mouth slightly agape.

"I didn't know it would be like this..." he says when I join him.

"You haven't been here? When you said you knew the place I assumed..."

"No, never. I have just walked past and seen the sign. I had no interest..."

He doesn't seem like someone with no interest now. The same thing that caught my attention has apparently stopped him in his tracks. He points at the frontal and translates.

"De meester is hier en roept voor u."

Really? Latin *and* English? Who is this guy?

"What does it mean? Is it from the Bible?"

"Yes, from the Gospel of John. The story of the raising of Lazarus. Do you know it?"

He shakes his head no, still staring at the frontal.

"Lazarus was a friend of Jesus. He had two sisters, Mary and Martha. When Lazarus dies, Jesus goes to visit them. These words are Martha's when she goes to summon her sister."

"Mary? Is that Mary Magdalene, the prostitute?"

It's always interesting to see what bits and pieces of the Bible float to the surface of secular culture. "Well, yes and no. No because John makes Mary Magdalene a character in her own right and clearly intends this Mary to be a separate person. But also yes because in the Middle Ages the church conflated..."

Thijs turns and looks at me, unsure of the word's meaning.

"Combined..."

He nods and turns back to the altar.

"Mary of Bethany—that's John's Mary—with Mary Magdalene and the 'sinful woman' who bathes Jesus's feet with her tears and dries them with her hair in the Gospel of Luke."

"'With her tears...'" Thijs repeats. "And Jesus allowed this? From a prostitute?"

"He did."

He is silent for a moment, processing this information. Then, with a slight shake of his head, he is ready to move on.

"*De monstrans.*"

"Yes."

We pass through the curtained doorway to the display cases and I indicate the object of our quest to him. He bends at the waist to examine it more closely, looking for all the world like a priest executing a solemn bow at Mass. He's so fully absorbed by the gold starburst that I find myself watching him instead of looking at it myself. After a moment he places the fingers of his right hand against the glass as though he wants to reach in and touch the finely worked metal. His hair falls into his eyes and he brushes it away with the same fingers, then puts them back on the glass. Satisfied at last, he stands up and asks me a question, still looking into the case.

"So the bread of the—what is it?—*het avondmaal.*"

"Communion."

"Of course. The communion bread is put in that glass circle?"

"Yes."

"Why?"

"It becomes an object of devotion for the faithful."

"What do they do?"

"They look at it on their knees, sing hymns, pray."

"And they believe they are looking at the body of Jesus?"

"Yes."

"But then they will eat his body?"

Questions like this make me crazy. I hate to choose between admitting that Christianity is a) confused or b) barbaric.

"Well, not at the same time. This bread is just to look at."

Thijs chortles. "For a discounted rate, I hope."

I am beginning to regret the connections I made between the monstrance and the window prostitutes. But as soon as he has made his joke, Thijs becomes solemn again. "I wonder if Jesus gets lonely in there, behind his window, forced to let people look at his body..."

Man, that's an interesting take on the veneration of the eucharist. Why have I never thought of it? For Thijs, the implications of Christian religious practice are lying right on the surface. An abyss of unexamined connections and collusions begins to open at my feet but closes again abruptly when the God-like voice of the docent comes over the P.A. system.

"*Het museum sluit. Iedereen alsjeblieft verlaten.* The museum is closing. Everyone please exit."

Thijs turns to me, anxious.

"I don't want to leave yet. I like it here."

"But it's closing. We have to."

"We can find some place."

"You mean hide?"

"Yes, of course."

"But I don't do things like that."

"Yes, I know, and you don't pick up fifteen-year-old boys, either."

"But you're not..."

"You weren't sure, though, were you?"

We return to the church. I hear footsteps coming up the stairs, probably the docent's, and I know all at once how Adam felt when God showed up in the garden to ask about that fruit. Thijs spots the confession booth and makes a beeline for it, dragging me by the elbow. He opens the door of the priest's compartment, pushes me inside and steps in after me, closing the door behind him.

The docent has come into the church. Thijs realizes we can be seen through the little window in the compartment's door, so he puts a hand on top of my head and pushes me down onto the shelf provided as a seat for the priest, then sits on my lap. This is not going to look good to the spurned man when he throws open the door and finds us.

But the spurned man does not throw open the door.

"Hello? Is anyone here?"

He doesn't repeat the question in Dutch, so I know he's on the prowl for me specifically. He hasn't seen Thijs and me leave the museum, so it stands to reason we must be here somewhere. He checks the room behind the altar with the display cases, and calls once more from the top of the back stairway.

"Is anyone down there?"

When he comes back into the church he still doesn't open the door to the confessional because he can't believe anyone would be that brazen. He and I have that in common.

Unable to find us or anyone else, the docent switches off the lights and heads downstairs. Thijs and I sit in silence for a moment, our breath gradually synchronizing. A faint scent of some spicy cologne mingles pleasantly with the smell of his leather jacket. I have to remind myself that we're hiding, not on a date, and keep my hands to myself.

When Thijs is convinced we're in the clear, he starts asking questions again, but now we both whisper.

"What is this thing we are in?"

"It's called a confessional. It's where people come to confess their sins to a priest."

"How does that work?"

"The person who is confessing sits on the other side of this window…"

I slide the cover back to reveal the grille I knew would be there.

"And the priest sits where we are and listens to the person's sins."

"I know that. I've seen it in movies. I meant how does it work to confess sins to a priest? What good does it do?"

"Oh. Well, there's the psychological benefit of getting them off your chest, I suppose."

"Really? That's it? You could go to a counselor for that."

He's making me uneasy again. I know what I'm supposed to say but I don't like how it's going to sound.

"No, that's not all. The priest is empowered by the church to absolve the sinner in the name of God."

"Absolve, what is that?"

"Forgive, wash away."

"Is that what the woman was doing with her tears? Washing away Jesus's sins?"

He's done it again. The church always reads that story as Jesus forgiving the woman her sins, but Thijs is right: *she's* doing the washing.

"Well, I'm not sure about Jesus's sins. Officially he doesn't have any."

Even in the gloom of the confessional I can see Thijs knit his brow at this.

"OK. Whatever. Do you have this power, to...to... absolve?"

I don't like where this is going.

"Yes..." I answer tentatively.

"Then I will confess."

The intimacy of our tiny chamber immediately turns claustrophobic.

"Really? Now? Do you think that's a good idea?"

"I do. My mother would say you are not a real priest and probably have no power to—absolve—but I am not a Christian so I suppose it doesn't matter."

Now I'm loaded for bear, and I also hate his mother.

"Do you want to move to the other side of the confessional and do this properly?"

"No."

"Why not?"

"This seems better. I am very comfortable here."

He flips his bang out of his eyes and stares at me in the darkness. For the first time since mouthing the words *thirty euros* he seems to be flirting with me. This will not be like any confession I've heard before.

"OK, shoot."

Thijs looks confused.

"Speak, I mean. I'm listening."

There is a long pause before he says anything. When he finally begins he turns his face away from me, and his words are slow and deliberate.

"When I was a child my father owned an ordinary travel agency. He arranged tickets and hotels for Dutch people to visit Rio or Sydney or San Francisco. When the internet came, he flipped his business the other way and began trying to get people to come to the Netherlands—for the tulips and the art, of course—but mostly for the sex. His business became very big, and he had to hire many more employees. When the government legalized prostitution, everything got turned on its head. All of a sudden the prostitutes had to register and they had to be over twenty-one. Well, many of the clients wanted younger, anonymous people. Then the government started closing down the brothels that didn't conform to the new laws, but the sex tourists kept coming. So Amsterdam needed new prostitutes. And it got them. My father and his colleagues in the travel industry saw to that."

"How do you know all this?"

Thijs gave a bitter laugh. "From my university. I was sitting in a political science class that was analyzing the relationship between the sex trade in the Netherlands and global human trafficking. The professor put a slide on the screen that followed the supply chain, from impoverished areas of the world to the travel industry to the women in the windows. Then she scrolled through a list of companies that were a part of that chain. My father's was on it."

"Geez."

"I felt ashamed. I hoped that no one else in the class knew my connection to what we'd just learned. No one did, but my own knowledge was bad enough."

"But surely it's your father who needs absolution, not you."

"Perhaps. But the money he makes out of De Wallen and its tourists pays for our home in *Oud-Zuid*—it is very lovely—and my education, my clothes, everything. I'm nineteen and I drive a Lamborghini. It's sick."

After a pause he continues.

"A month after I found out the truth I began coming here to the district again and again. I wanted to connect with the sex workers, figure out a way to work together against my father's interests. People just laughed at me. I learned that everyone in De Wallen only wants to make their money: the *raamprostituees*, their pimps, the syndicates the pimps report to. It is essential that the money flow constantly, without interruption. I was just an annoyance to most, but a bit of a threat to others. That's when I learned that the *Rosse Buurt* is really a very dangerous place."

He turns to face me again. His lips are so close to my cheek that I can feel his breath on my face, and each word seems to write itself on my skin.

"You must always do whatever a person who does not value human life and has a gun in his hand tells you to do."

I feel a chill go through my body. What has Thijs been asked—or forced—to do at gunpoint? I feel an urge to protect him from something that has already happened, change the course of his story. He turns away from me once again and continues speaking into the dry, dusty air of the confessional.

"One pimp laid out for me exactly how much money I could make if I worked for him, way more than anyone my age ever makes. If I'd needed the money we might have made a bargain."

"So you haven't actually..."

"No. I tried a few times, a misguided attempt at solidarity, but no one took me seriously. Except the man downstairs, but I ran the other way as soon as I pictured his hands on me. Sitting here with you is the farthest I've ever gotten with anyone who thought I was for sale. You were the first person stupid enough to think a rent boy would wear Prada."

"Hey!"

A faint smile comes and goes quickly on Thijs' lips.

"In spite of my lack of success as a prostitute I thought I could shock my father into changing his ways by making him think I'd become one. So I told him I now had a pimp and was working out of a high-end sex club. He just laughed at me and wished me good luck."

"Really? He's that cruel?"

"No. He knows me that well. He could tell I was...what is that word? Bluffing. He sees nothing wrong with the way he makes money. He's not a bad person. He just chooses not to look very closely at how the world really works."

"Very few people do, Thijs."

He gives no sign of hearing me.

"And now I am quite unsure how the rest of my life will unfold. I have thought about giving everything I own back to my father..."

"Like Saint Francis..."

"Who?"

"Never mind."

"...and leaving the university he pays for. But what would I really accomplish? My father and his colleagues would continue to pour money into human trafficking, and nothing in De Wallen would change. My father would probably even commend me for my integrity. Because he knows that I will come round in the end."

Thijs shifts his weight on my lap and arches his back, stretching his spine and pressing his buttocks down harder against my thigh. I struggle to stay in confessor mode.

"Maybe I'm just going through my righteous university student phase, when everyone thinks they will save the world their parents have fucked up. Maybe I like nice things more than I admit to myself. Maybe I will agree to look the other way so I can go on having those things, like my father."

He is sounding bitter again, the way he had on *Oudekerksplein* when we passed the statue of Belle. The anguish in his voice throws cold water on my salacious thoughts.

"You know, I don't even believe there is a God, but if there were I know that He would never look away. *He would never look away.*"

His voice begins to rise, and I hope the docent has gone home.

"He would see that Bulgarian woman who thought she was coming to work in a hotel and has no money or friends or even a phone to help her escape, and that Asian boy who applied to work as a busboy and now spends his days making old men cum in their pants when he's not lost in a drugged-up haze. And he would see me, wearing Prada paid for by the Bulgarian woman and the Asian boy, and by you, for that matter, if I'd been what you thought I was. But you know what? The idea that God sees everything only helps for about five minutes until you realize He's not going to *do* anything about what he sees, He *can't* do anything, because He is stuck in a *monstrans*, trapped by gold and diamonds, and all He can do is watch as we make a shit-pile of the world he gave us. So, really, why should I care if He forgives me or not? It's all just *stront.*"

In the fading spring sunlight that barely pierces the gloom of the confessional I can see tears streaming quietly down Thijs' face. He puts his head against my chest and the tears turn to quiet sobs. I wrap my arms around him, this boy-man I have known for less than three hours, and gently rock him back and forth, wondering what the hell to say. One cliché after another forms in my mind and gets rejected. I think back to the lecture he gave me when we were standing in the street—it feels like a lifetime ago. His bitterness and indignation make sense to me now. As far as I'm concerned he has no need of absolution, but surely he deserves some kind of comfort.

"Thijs, if you feel a need to confess that you and your family benefit from the sex trade, you're just being honest. More honest than I am, more than a lot of people. A lot of the world is what you said...a shit-pile, but that isn't God's fault. It's ours. This is how we treat each other."

He is quiet now, listening to me. I stroke his hair as I continue.

"One thing I'm quite sure of, though. Without any religion you are living better than most Christians I know, all those millions of people worshiping Jesus and eating his body and feeling satisfied that they're on God's good side. But they don't see what you see, and, because you see it, you will make the world better. I'm sure of it."

I slide my thumb under his bang and gently trace a cross on the smooth skin of his forehead. Then I say the words I'm supposed to say, the words the church has authorized me to say: "The Lord has put away all your sins. Go in peace, and pray for me, a sinner."

Thijs sits up and looks at my face for a long moment. Then he lifts one hand and gently strokes my face.

"Thank you," he says, almost tenderly. "That was the perfect thing to say."

Without thinking I turn my head and kiss his palm. That's all it takes. He puts one hand behind my head and pulls me toward him, covering my mouth with his own and kissing me harder than I've ever been kissed. His lips feel surprisingly firm as he works my mouth expertly, and so pleasurably that I worry I may climax on the spot. But as abruptly as the kiss began, it's over. Thijs pulls away from me and takes a handkerchief out of his back pocket to blot his mouth.

"And now may I have my thirty euros?

"What?"

"My thirty euros. Surely you agree that I have earned it."

I am almost too stunned to speak.

"*Earned* it?" I manage to blurt out. "But...but we didn't do anything! And besides, I thought you...I thought *we*...what exactly am I paying you for?"

He looks at me like I'm an idiot.

"For the *performance*, of course. I had fun. I hope you did, too. Something a bit different."

The wealthy, compromised father, the Lamborghini, the earnest young penitent—all the vivid images Thijs has conjured over the past half hour shatter into tiny pieces and pile up at my feet. I replay the afternoon in fast motion, trying to find something definite, some *fact* I can use to reorient myself, but there's not a single one. Even the driver's license was probably a fake.

From somewhere in the distance the rhythmic shriek of a police siren snaps me out of my fog. I see that Thijs has pulled out a small revolver, which he is pointing at me. I assume at first that it's a toy, but the icy expression on his face assures me that I'm wrong about that.

"Hurry, please. It seems *de winkelbediende* has called the police. What I told you about him is not true. Well, almost nothing I told you is true. He's one of my best customers, so he was very unhappy to see me with you. I'm sure he was even more unhappy that I showed up at his precious museum with a client. For that he will try to have me arrested. You, too, perhaps. He is a bitter man, with many grudges." Thijs laughs again at the stupid English word.

My hands tremble badly as I take out my wallet and hand him the same forty euros he waved in my face when we first met. Thijs looks down at the bills and then up at me. Hoping I don't sound as scared as I feel, I say: "Consider it a tip."

"*Een fooi*? Excellent."

Fooi? That's the Dutch word for tip? Talk about a stupid word. Yet somehow appropriate for the occasion.

He slides the gun back inside his jacket and then places the money neatly in his billfold.

"For future reference, try to remember this. Teenagers from the *Oud-Zuid* do not prowl *De Wallen* to atone for their sins, and if you think anything I'm wearing was made by Prada then you deserve never to own any yourself."

He opens the door of the confessional and hops off my lap. I discover that I have no feeling in my legs, and that is really unfortunate, because the sirens have reached the museum and stopped.

"Come with me now. Hurry!"

He runs across the dim church and darts through the doorway to the left of the altar. I follow as quickly as I can but I'm moving like someone who's just gotten off a boat. By the time I reach the display room he's already cantering down the back stairs two at a time. He waits for me to catch up with him at the bottom, where there's a door marked with big red letters:

NOODOUITGANG

Thijs, or whatever the hell his name is, throws his weight against the crash bar and suddenly we are in the alley, a deafening alarm bell clanging in our ears. There in his right hand is the monstrance, its diamonds glinting jauntily in the setting sun.

"It is a wonderful piece. Thank you for bringing it to my attention."

OK, now I've abetted a burglary in addition to soliciting a teenager. I briefly consider grabbing the monstrance to return it to the museum, but that conversation could not possibly go well, and there's always the gun, so I try to reason with him.

"You said the...the...*vinkelbedoonder*...whatever...knows you. How do you expect to get away with this?"

"By the time the police come to question me it will be long gone—liberated of its diamonds, of course. And it may be some time before they come, since he doesn't know my real name any more than you do. They will find you before they find me. So I suggest you get as far away as you possibly can, as quickly as you can. *Dag!*"

He tosses the monstrance into his rucksack and takes off down the alley.

"But..."

He stops and twists his torso to look at me, clearly impatient.

"Will I see you again?"

This guy just pulled a gun on me and I want a second date? Sadly, yes.

"You should hope that you do not. I'm not always in such a playful mood. Goodbye, *mijnheer pastoor*."

With that he disappears around a corner. Taking the master's advice to heart I turn and run in the opposite direction. The sound of the museum's alarm continues to resound in my head long after I'm too far away to hear it.

I Am the Rose of Sharon

HI, MY NAME IS **K**yle.

Kyle pinned the white badge onto the top of his green apron as soon as the ink had dried and handed the marker back to his manager.

"Really? That's the best you could do?" asked Gary. He'd brought the name tags back from a convention. "They're supposed to stimulate your creativity."

"Give me a break," said Kyle. "I mean, who ever has to *write* their name?"

He'd made the K too big and had to squeeze the remaining letters in as best he could. After looking at the result he'd decided to underline it for emphasis, but that was it. He hoped Gary wasn't going to ask him to start dressing creatively, too. He liked wearing the same black jeans and belt and a white button-down shirt with the sleeves rolled up to his elbows every day. He figured his apron covered most of him up anyway. A creative haircut would be a deal-breaker, too. Kyle was morally opposed to barbershops, which meant he had to push his thick brown curls out of his eyes with some regularity.

Douglas though that gesture was the most perfect thing he had ever seen another human being do.

Kyle was twenty years old and worked as a cashier at the Hy-Vee supermarket in Algona, Iowa, where Douglas was his best customer, a fact Kyle was oblivious to. Douglas was sixty-two and worked from home, taking calls forwarded to him by a phone center in Indonesia from people in the United States who wanted to enter a sweepstakes giveaway. His job was to enroll them in the sweepstakes and then try to sell them magazines at "amazing" discounts if they didn't hang up, which they usually did. A trip to the grocery store was a welcome distraction from the tedium of his work, so he went early and often. Once he'd found his apple juice or Graham crackers he would loiter nonchalantly near the checkout, pretending to shop the gift card display, until Kyle's line was free and he could be sure another cashier wouldn't invite him to step over.

Douglas was thrilled when he saw Kyle's new badge because it gave a name to the object of his affection. As far as he was concerned, the sloppiness gave it an added charm, He wanted to respond "Hi, Kyle, my name is Douglas," but he was too shy. Invisible, too, apparently, because in spite of the fact that he bought one or more grocery items from Kyle almost every day, the younger man never gave the slightest indication of recognizing him.

+   +   +

At first Douglas tried to convince himself that Kyle suffered from that neurological problem that makes people unable to distinguish faces, but he seemed to know his other customers quite well and chatted with them easily, sometimes flashing a smile that displayed fetchingly imperfect teeth. Yet whenever it was Douglas's turn Kyle was invariably all business, sometimes nodding perfunctorily in Douglas's direction or muttering a listless "Hi," but just as often saying nothing as he dragged each item across the scanner and dropped it into the plastic bag hanging from the little metal frame behind him. Douglas longed for the tiniest bit of give-and-take, but had to settle for those ecstatic seconds when Kyle brushed the hair away from his eyes and he could see their liquidy brown depths.

Of course, if Kyle had ever turned those pretty eyes directly on his best customer and asked him how his day was going, Douglas wouldn't have known what to do. An anxious only child, he'd lived with his mother and father till he was fifty, then alone with his widowed mother until her passing two years ago. The comfortable familiarity of his childhood home and bedroom helped him manage his anxiety, which had persisted and increased in spite of counseling and medication, keeping him out the workplace and preventing any kind of a normal social life. The only time he interacted with anyone besides his mother was when he took her to church on Sundays, but since her death he just stayed home and read his Bible.

Douglas had never felt about anyone the way he felt about Kyle, and three months after seeing him for the first time his visits to the grocery store had become the organizing principle of his daily life. This fact was not lost on Gary, who had decided that Douglas was a problem.

"Doesn't it seem like that guy's in here a lot? I mean, more than he needs to be?"

Mel, the assistant manager, was reviewing the cashiers' schedule for the coming week. He glanced at Douglas standing in the checkout line.

"Yeah, I think he's hot for Kyle."

"I thought it was something like that. Disgusting." He shuddered. "I don't think that's appropriate behavior for a family grocery store."

"Well, don't let the P.C. types hear you," Mel chuckled. "We might get in trouble."

Gary scowled as he continued to glare at Douglas from the customer service booth. "Don't get me going," he muttered.

When his shift ended that night Gary phoned his wife to say he'd be a little late for dinner. Then he combed through the security camera tapes from the past week, hoping to find evidence to nail this guy. Evidence of what specific crime or store policy violation, he could not put into exact words, because the depravity of *those people* seemed both bottomless and (thankfully) vague. But he was sure he'd know it when he saw it.

+   +   +

In spite of being a church dropout Douglas knew his Bible well. Throughout his life he had inscribed scripture verses on index cards and left them anonymously for people he liked, hoping they'd be cheered and encouraged when they found them. For the librarian who always let him check out more books than the library's limit, he'd written: *The one who conquers will be clothed thus in white garments, and I will never blot his name out of the book of life: Revelation 3:5.* And for the owner of Ma and Pa's Country Candy Store who kept a secret stash of Maple Nut Goodies so that Douglas would never have to go home disappointed, he chose: *My son, eat thou honey, because it is good; and the honeycomb, which is sweet to thy taste: Proverbs 24:13.* He'd slip the cards onto the counter or under a blotter when no one was looking and leave quickly, before they could be found. Sometimes a recipient would tack the verse to a bulletin board or tape it to the cash register for everyone to see, which made Douglas feel like he'd done a good thing. Now he wanted to make a card for Kyle, but delivering it would be a challenge, since Kyle never left his cash register. If he just handed it to him Kyle would know who it was from, and Douglas didn't want that. Besides, what would he say? *Here are some Bible verses...they made me think of you?* Kyle would throw them out and look at Douglas like he was crazy.

Then it came to him. If he put Kyle's name on the card, he could just drop it in the general vicinity without having to identify himself as the giver. Kyle might not find it till the end of his shift when he tidied up for his replacement. And even if the next cashier found it, they could still deliver it because it would have Kyle's name on it. Yes, that was the solution. Now to choose the verses.

Douglas knew just where to look—The Song of Solomon, the love poem sandwiched between Ecclesiastes and Isaiah which the pastor had steadfastly refused to discuss in Bible study. He quickly found the words he wanted to praise Kyle's beauty:

> My beloved is white and ruddy, the chiefest among ten thousand.
> His head is as the most fine gold, his locks are bushy, and black as a raven.

Douglas squirmed with delight. Kyle's locks were indeed bushy, even if they were brown and not black. He usually wrote only a single verse, but there was too much good material to stop there.

> His eyes are the eyes of doves by the rivers of waters, washed with milk and fitly set.
> His cheeks are as a bed of spices, as sweet flowers his lips like lilies, dropping sweet smelling myrrh.
> His hands are as gold rings set with the beryl; his belly is as bright ivory overlaid with sapphires.

Douglas blushed at the thought of Kyle's belly, an image he would not have contemplated without the scripture's encouragement. It was probably covered in fine reddish-gold hair, like his forearms. Picturing it made him feel a little queasy, so he stopped.

>*His legs are as pillars of marble, set upon sockets of fine gold;*
>*his countenance is as Lebanon, excellent as the cedars.*

The last bit made Douglas think of the wooden Indian that used to stand outside the tobacco store when he was a kid; he'd skip that one.

>*His mouth is most sweet; yea, he is altogether lovely.*

"Perfect," Douglas said aloud. He'd end on "altogether lovely." But then his eye roamed across the page and alighted on the opening verse of Chapter 2:

>*I am the rose of Sharon, and the lily of the valleys.*

Too good to leave out. He'd work that in, too. He now had far too many verses for an index card (*Unless I want it to look like Kyle's name tag,* he thought with a snort). He'd need a full sheet of paper. He found some vellum stationery in his mother's top desk drawer and took a sheet to his bedroom, where he laid it on the pristine surface of his own desk. He smoothed the paper carefully with his hand and thought about the fact that the next hand to touch it would be Kyle's. He sat down, took out his fountain pen, and wrote:

Dear Kyle,

He saw at once that this would be an altogether different kind of gift from his anonymous index cards. This was going to be a letter—a letter to Kyle from God!—and Douglas would be a kind of emissary, like the angel who told the Virgin Mary she was going to have a baby. In a second burst of inspiration he decided to make the verses sound like God was speaking directly to Kyle:

Your head is as the most fine gold...your eyes are as the eyes of doves by the rivers of waters...you are altogether lovely.

Yes, this was going to work! Unlike Kyle, Douglas wrote in longhand every day, and when he took his time his handwriting was almost as pretty as calligraphy. He finished with the "extra" verse from Chapter 2:

You are the rose of Sharon, and the lily of the valleys.

How true that was! Douglas understood that he would never see his gift received, much less be thanked for it, but that wasn't the point. He just wanted Kyle to know how beautiful he was, and how much he—no, God—loved him. To be sure that point got across he signed the letter with a flourish:

God

He folded the letter carefully in three, returned to his mother's desk for an envelope, and put the finished product on the tray near the door for outgoing mail. He had more trouble than usual going to sleep that night, anticipating the letter's delivery in the morning.

+   +   +

Douglas did a full week's shopping at the Hy-Vee the next day, ensuring that he'd have a good long time in Kyle's line to deliver the letter when he wasn't looking. He held the envelope in his hand as he walked up and down the aisles, glancing at it from time to time so people would think it was a grocery list. He was anxious about the success of his mission, but not so anxious that he couldn't savor the last moments before he made his gift of God's beautiful words to Kyle. To prolong his happiness he kept adding things to his cart that he didn't need or couldn't actually use, like charcoal briquets, and a box of Stay-Free Mini-Pads.

At 10 AM sharp Douglas decided the moment had come. There were only a few shoppers in the store, so he was able to nose his cart into Kyle's lane with no waiting. The young man's face was hidden behind a copy of *The National Enquirer*, but when the first of Douglas's items glided down the conveyor belt into his line of vision he closed the paper and stuck it back in the rack. Without greeting Douglas, he began scanning the groceries with dismaying efficiency, quickly reducing delivery time for the letter to a brief window. To make matters worse, another cashier wandered over to bag, a wrinkle Douglas had not anticipated. What if she saw him leave the letter? Douglas began to despair. Soon he had only one item left on the conveyor belt, a case of bottled water, and when it was scanned he'd have to pay and go home. Sadly, he decided he'd have to deliver the letter another day.

Then fortune smiled on him.

Kyle couldn't find the UPC code on the water. He bent over the case to see if it was in front, thrusting the top of his head practically into Douglas's face. Douglas felt an overwhelming urge to lean in a little and see what the tousled brown hair smelled like. Did he dare? It was only a matter of an inch or two. The other cashier had finished bagging and gone back to her station. He looked behind him...no one in line. His heart racing, he closed his eyes, leaned forward, and gently inhaled. At the same moment, Kyle flipped the bottles on their side and turned his head to look at them from that angle, sweeping his curls right across Douglas's face.

The older man recoiled violently. He felt dizzy, like he might faint. He mustn't faint! What could he do? He gripped the edge of the counter so hard his knuckles turned white; he took short, quick breaths to try to slow his rapid pulse. The sensation of Kyle's hair on his face had been terrible and wonderful at the same time, the most intimate encounter he'd ever had with another human being.

And he had had it alone.

"Can't find a price on these...I'll have to go check. Hang on."

Kyle lifted the hinged counter that boxed him into his station and trotted off to the bottled water aisle at the far end of the store. In his absence Douglas's breath began to return to normal. He was glad Kyle hadn't noticed what just happened, but sorry that he hadn't had a chance to prepare for the moment. He wanted to remember every detail of it— the scent of lemony shampoo mingled with something more pungent and herbal, like sage, the incredible softness of the hair punctuated by the distinct firmness of the curls—but it was fading already.

Douglas suddenly remembered the letter. Where was it? He had dropped it the moment Kyle's hair swept over his face! It lay on the floor at his feet. He stooped and picked it up, took a quick look around, and slid it under Kyle's cash register drawer, leaving just an inch of the cream-colored envelope showing. Then he perused the chewing gum selection until Kyle returned.

"On special," Kyle said, pivoting gracefully back into place and punching $4.99 into the keyboard. "Your lucky day!"

Kyle looked Douglas right in the eye and smiled, absently pushing his bang out of the way.

"That'll be $106.77."

The smile was gone by the time Kyle handed Douglas's credit card back to him, and no further communication ensued, not even a "thank you." Douglas wanted to volunteer something to prolong their time together but didn't trust himself not to sound foolish, so he took his receipt and pushed the shopping cart toward the door.

Gary was waiting for him.

"I need to speak with you."

Douglas looked as startled as he felt. No one ever needed to speak with him, except his bosses in Indonesia, and even that was pretty rare.

"I'm the manager here, and I've been watching you."

Douglas gulped. This couldn't be happening.

"You're here a lot, pretty much every day. But you never go to a single cashier besides Kyle."

At the sound of Kyle's name Douglas began to panic. What did this man know? Was he going to be arrested? What had he done?

"It's all on our security camera tapes. You hang around waiting for Kyle's lane to be free. That's not a normal shopper."

Speech had left Douglas. He could only stare at Gary in terror.

"I think you need to find yourself another grocery store. Because if I see you in here again I'll report you to the police. And you know what happens then to guys like you? Your name gets put on the sex offender registry, that's what. And you won't be able to live near schools—or grocery stores, in your case—and somebody will be keeping an eye on you and your sick behavior night and day. So consider yourself warned."

Gary narrowed his eyes and lifted his chin defiantly toward Douglas, signifying dismissal. Douglas staggered toward the sliding doors, leaving his groceries sitting in the shopping cart. He wanted to run but his knees felt weak.

Mel came out of the customer service booth. "Oh, for heaven's sake, what'd you wanna go and do that for? The guy's harmless. We need all the customers we can get these days."

"Not that one," Gary said grimly. He walked over to Kyle, who had resumed reading the tabloid.

"Did that man bother you, Kyle?"

"Who?"

"That…weirdo who just checked out. Did he say anything inappropriate to you?"

Kyle looked out the window at the parking lot and saw Douglas hurrying to his car. He dropped his keys on the ground, retrieved them with shaking hands, then got in and sped away.

"No, I don't think so," he said. "I've never seen him before."

+   +   +

Kyle's shift ended at 4:30. He signed out of his register and pulled the cash drawer from its slot. Douglas's envelope fell to the floor, unnoticed, as he let himself out of the station and carried the till to Mel. Marie, a woman with unnaturally bright red hair whom Kyle estimated to be at least a hundred years old, took his place.

"Good afternoon, Kyle," she said as they passed one another.

"Hi, Marie. Enjoy yourself."

"Always do."

Kyle handed the drawer across the service desk to Mel, who acknowledged it with a nod.

"Anything fun on tonight?"

Mel felt bad that Kyle's father wasn't around, so he tried to supply a little paternal interest from time to time.

"Nah, nothing special. Just parkour."

"Say what? Parcheesi? Aren't you a little old for board games?"

Kyle was really tired of that question.

"No, parkour. It's a kind of...sport, I guess. Some people call it free running. You run from Point A to Point B in the most efficient way possible, but there are, like, obstacles in between, so you have to—you know—navigate them."

"I don't get it. Why not just take the bus?"

Kyle had learned that people unfamiliar with parkour either thought it was the coolest thing they'd ever heard of, or a complete waste of time.

"It's not meant to be practical. It's more of an art form, I guess."

"Huh. Are there girls involved?"

Kyle looked down at his shoes. He'd seen the joke circulating on the internet: "Parkour? Nah, I've got a girlfriend."

"Um, not really."

Mel put a hand on Kyle's shoulder and squeezed it gently.

"Don't worry, it's not you. I find my own kids just as confusing. Have a good time."

"Yeah, thanks, Mel. I will."

Kyle hung the green apron in his locker in the tiny employee lounge behind the service desk and threw his leather jacket on. He pulled his car keys out of a pocket and returned to the store, heading for the exit.

"Kyle!"

Marie was waving a piece of paper at him from the cash register.

"Did you mean to leave this? Has your name on it."

Kyle shrugged and walked over to take the envelope from Marie's hand. There, indeed, was his name, written in elegant cursive letters. He wished he could have made his badge look like that.

Marie had no customer at the moment and couldn't suppress her curiosity.

"What do you think it is?"

"No idea."

He turned it over but found no clues to the sender. Whatever it was, he wasn't going to open it in front of Marie.

"A love letter, maybe? From a secret admirer?"

Kyle knitted his brows.

"I doubt it."

"Well, I wouldn't be surprised. If I were twenty years younger..."

Kyle looked up, startled by the direction the conversation had taken. Marie misinterpreted his gesture.

"OK, forty years younger...I'd probably make a play for you myself. Those puppy-dog eyes...women are a sucker for 'em."

Kyle turned his head away just in time to prevent Marie catching his puppy-dog eyes roll. "Thanks, Marie."

Kyle walked to the electric-blue '99 Corolla at the edge of the parking lot, a hand-me-down from his dad. He got in and closed the door, then placed the envelope on the center of the steering wheel. He wasn't sure he wanted to open it. He tried to think of someone he knew who might want to communicate with him this way. He couldn't remember the last time anyone had written him a letter, unless you counted birthday cards from out-of-town relatives who were near death. But those usually had money in them. What if this did, too? He stuck his finger under the flap and ripped it open.

Dear Kyle,

    Your eyes are the eyes of doves by the rivers of waters, washed with milk and fitly set. Your cheeks are as a bed of spices, as sweet flowers your lips like lilies, dropping sweet smelling myrrh.

"What the fuck?" he said, half aloud.

He quickly scanned the rest of the letter, thinking its meaning might become clearer at some point. It didn't.

Your mouth is most sweet; yea, you are altogether lovely.
You are the rose of Sharon, and the lily of the valleys.

And then came the real kicker, the signature.

God

Kyle dropped the letter in his lap and looked around the parking lot. Was he being punked? Were his friends out there somewhere with a camera, hoping to post his reaction on Instagram? He didn't see anyone in the immediate vicinity. He read the letter through one more time, then tossed it and the envelope onto the passenger seat. The whole way home he made a point of not looking at it.

A few blocks from his house his phone pinged. He pulled it out of his jacket pocket and saw a text from his friend Logan:

Run 2nt @8. RU UP4IT?

K, he replied, looking from the road to his phone as his thumb moved rapidly over the keypad.

M & J 2?

UNOIT, Logan fired back.

K, CUL8R

A SMILE IN EVERY AISLE (This was the Hy-Vee grocery chain's motto and a favorite taunt of Logan's.)

BIOYA

SRY. A HELPFUL SMILE IN EVERY AISLE

BIOYAX2

Kyle parked next to his mother's car in the driveway. He picked up the letter from the passenger seat, put it in the envelope without looking at it, and shoved it into his back pocket as he got out of the car. He dragged the empty garbage cans from the curb into the garage and closed the overhead door. His little brother appeared in the doorway to the laundry room. Benjamin was eight going on eighteen.

"Hi, Kyle."

"Hi, squirt. What'd you learn in school today?"

"The state flag of Iowa was designed by a woman named Dixie Gebhardt. She lived from 1866 to 1955. It has an eagle in the middle, and the eagle is holding the state motto on a ribbon in its mouth."

"Is that so?"

Kyle brushed past Benjamin into the family room and threw his jacket on the sofa. He wondered if he had learned facts like that in second grade. Mostly he remembered making ugly papier-mâché sculptures.

"The state motto is 'Our liberties we prize and our rights we will maintain.'"

"Well, everybody knows that."

Kyle went into the kitchen and pulled a bag of Cheetos out of a cabinet. He shoved a handful into his mouth and thought about what to cook for dinner that night. Benjamin had followed him and had more to say.

"Mrs. Gebhardt felt very strongly about flags. She said 'Flags are symbols of the achievements of the human race.'"

"Man, you're sure getting your money's worth out of our tax dollars, squirt."

Benjamin frowned, not sure if his brother was making fun of him.

"Don't call me 'squirt.'"

Kyle took some ground beef out of the freezer and put it in the microwave to thaw.

"OK, squirt. I won't, squirt. I'm very sorry, squirt."

Benjamin laughed in spite of himself. Kyle tweaked his little brother's nose and went down the hall to his bedroom. He paused outside his mother's closed door.

"Mom? I'm home."

"OK," she replied, sounding distracted. "I think you're cooking dinner tonight. Do you?"

"Yes."

Kyle's mother was a secretary at a law office in town, but she was taking classes online to become a paralegal, so she spent a lot of her time at home on the computer in her bedroom.

Kyle went into his room and locked the door. He flopped down on the bed and opened the letter again. He'd once found a flyer stuck on his car's windshield advertising something called "End of Times Ministries." It had a picture of two people who looked like Roy Rogers and Dolly Parton who wanted to warn him about the imminent collapse of the world's economy due to a conspiracy between the Vatican and Israel. It claimed that Kyle could hear a message from God just for him if he would call the number printed below and donate ten dollars or more to the ministry. Was this letter like that? Not really. There was no request for money. And this in fact seemed to *be* a message from God, *just for him*, but that was crazy thinking.

He jumped off the bed, crossed the room to the laptop lying open on his desk and Googled *Your mouth is most sweet; yea, you are altogether lovely*. Up popped several thousand porn and dating sites.

Better try a different line. He typed: *You are the rose of Sharon, and the lily of the valleys*.

This time every result included the words "Song of Songs 2:1" or "Song of Solomon 2:1." He thought it was a piece of music until he clicked on a couple of the entries and learned the "song" was a book of the Bible. But the line wasn't supposed to be *You are the rose of Sharon*; it was *I am the rose of Sharon*. In a short time he had located every one of the letter's phrases in that same book, all of them changed to become descriptions of Kyle.

He leaned back in his chair and tried to reason his way to the identity of the author. Who would know a lot of Bible shit? Especially all this kind of steamy stuff, which wasn't like anything Kyle had thought was in the Bible. Whoever wrote it seemed to be hot for him. He hoped she was a babe. He ran through the catalogue of his female acquaintances. Patty Smolz was always carrying a Bible around when they were in high school. She had great tits, Kyle remembered, but that Bible seemed like some kind of warning not to look at them. Besides, Patty got married and moved to Sioux City. Whoever wrote this was still in Algona.

Joyce Kelly? Her father owned the Chevy dealership, and they had kind of kept in touch since high school, but she was dating a guy from Mason City the last he knew. Amy Terhune? He was pretty sure she was a dyke. Pam Grimaldi? Kathy Thiessen? Sally Lewan? They were all Facebook friends but he hadn't seen any of them in person since high school unless they came to the store, and then they'd just say hi. Besides, they were all pretty normal, and this letter seemed definitely the opposite.

Christ, what if it was Marie? She'd produced the thing out of nowhere, after all, and as much as told him she had a crush on him. But no, she had a husband and grandchildren, and she was known to throw a few back on the weekends. It definitely wasn't her. Kyle was getting a headache thinking about it. He crumpled up the letter and tossed it into the wastebasket under his desk, then went to work culinary magic with a box of Hamburger Helper.

Thirty minutes later the family gathered around the kitchen table. Annie, Kyle's mother, was a viable forty-two-year-old with blonde highlights in her light brown hair and a vaguely Holly-Hunterish kind of pixie face. His sister Christine could pass for her mother's younger sister. She played first clarinet in her high school orchestra and had won a music scholarship to Oberlin College, where she would start classes in the fall. Then there was Benjamin, the boy genius, with a perpetual old man's expression on his otherwise cute eight year-old's face. He'd probably be a nuclear physicist by sixteen. As Kyle watched his family help themselves to Cheesy Ranch Burger Noodles, broccoli, and garlic bread, he noted, not for the first time, that he was definitely the underachiever of the group. Parkour wasn't exactly a career path.

"So are you running tonight?" Annie asked.

The question pleased Kyle. Initially his mother had been one of the people who confused parkour with parcheesi.

"As a matter of fact, I am. We all are. Logan, Josh, Martin and me."

"Martin and I," said Christine, who had filled her plate with broccoli and only a spoonful of casserole and a single corner of garlic bread. "Are we ever going to see a demonstration?"

Kyle massaged the callouses on his palms under the table, thinking of all the times he'd wiped out.

"Um, sure...when we're good enough."

"You've been doing it for three years now...how long does it take?"

"Christine, don't be snotty to your brother. He works hard all day and if this is how he likes to relax, let him enjoy it."

"I wasn't being snotty. I really want to know how long it takes."

"Well, how long does it take to be a good clarinetist?" Kyle asked.

"Really? You're saying that running around an obstacle course is the same as becoming a professional musician?"

"You're saying it isn't? You know, I've been to every one of your damn orchestra concerts, even though I was bored out of mind."

"*Kyle*! Watch your language."

"And your point is..."

"Well, how about a little support from your side? Maybe you *should* come and watch us some time. It might just be that you're not the only artist in the family."

"Just tell me when," Christine said primly. "You won't have to ask twice."

"Tell me, too!" shouted Benjamin, who found the tension between his older siblings thrilling.

Kyle looked at his little brother and laughed.

"OK, squirt. We'll make it a family outing."

"Yay!"

As soon as dinner was over Annie returned to her studies, Christine gathered up the plates to load them into the dishwasher, and Benjamin sat down in front of the TV to watch SpongeBob reruns and read a book about spiders. Kyle got into his car and headed out to pick up his friends.

It had been one of those limp early April days that wasn't quite winter but felt nothing like spring. The sun was glowing feebly behind a bank of gray clouds on the horizon as Kyle headed across town to Logan's house. His sister's words came back into his mind—*you've been doing it for three years now*—and he realized she'd actually been paying attention. It was almost exactly three years ago that he and Josh and Logan were sitting in that study hall together, bored out of their minds. When the teacher got up to go to the bathroom Martin whispered, "Look at this" and showed them Sébastien Foucan's "Jump London" video on his iPad. Their mouths were soon gaping as they watched guys their age hurtle through the streets of London, then over its rooftops and famous monuments, leaping across the chasms between buildings, somersaulting off walls, balancing on concrete pylons and embankments, sometimes on their feet, sometimes on their hands, all accompanied by a pounding rock soundtrack which Martin had all but muted. It was kind of like breakdancing, kind of like gymnastics, maybe even a little like ballet, all wrapped up in a six-minute mile. "It's called parkour," Martin said reverently. It was obviously pure insanity, and they knew instantly it was going to be their insanity from then on.

"Hey," said Logan as he slid into the passenger seat.

"Hey," said Kyle. "What's the latest?"

Logan turned and looked out the window as the houses in his neighborhood passed by.

"Not good, not good. Lots of drama tonight. Glad to be with you guys."

Logan's parents were divorcing. Kyle's dad had left without warning three years ago.

"Don't worry, it gets better."

"Yeah, if you're *gay*. Where's the YouTube channel for straight boys with crazy parents? I'd watch that."

Martin had dinner at Josh's house, so they were both standing at the curb as Kyle pulled up.

"Hey, guys," said Logan as they clambered into the cramped back seat, trying not to sit on one of the many empty pop cans. "What culinary extravaganza did you partake of this evening?"

"Josh's mother is an amazing cook, let me tell you. Ain't nobody can hold a candle to the way that woman pops a frozen pizza in the oven."

"What a jerk! Why do I invite you over? Why do you come? You are a bad guest, Martin Haverdale, you know that? Besides, she made a salad from scratch."

"Yeah, with bottled dressing and Bac-os. What do you think those things are made of? I wonder if they cause cancer?"

"Oh, just shut the fuck up."

"It's touching to see good friends enjoying each other's company, isn't it, Kyle?"

"I agree."

Kyle pulled into the parking lot of the shuttered U-Store-It and headed for the back of the building, where he could leave the car out of sight from the road. The building had been a shoe factory that closed before they were born. After two decades somebody who'd heard that self-storage facilities were the Next Big Thing bought it and brought in sturdy cartons of all sizes, some as big as rooms, and gave the place a thorough cleaning. Unfortunately, the new owners failed to take into account that a town of 5600 practical Iowans had little to store and preferred throwing things out to paying to keep them somewhere else. The business was in receivership and everyone seemed to have forgotten about it. Somebody, some time would come and collect the cartons, but for now it was all theirs. No more kiddie playgrounds, no more jaywalking tickets from policemen with too little real crime to keep themselves busy.

By shoving the storage cartons into groups and making use of the existing ramps and railings of the old factory the boys had created a first-rate urban landscape completely hidden from prying eyes. Each week one of them would select a soundtrack and choreograph a new routine to its rhythms, outlining new paths through the many obstacles in their way and suggesting the most challenging moves to transcend them. They'd walk through the course in slow motion, then blast the music and run it for real. Hand-painted placards around the room shouted their favorite parkour mottoes:

DON'T THINK THE MOVEMENT: BE THE MOVEMENT

THE FIRST RULE OF FOCUS IS THIS: WHEREVER YOU ARE, BE THERE.

IF YOU KEEP DOING THINGS LIKE YOU'VE ALWAYS DONE THEM, WHAT YOU'LL GET IS WHAT YOU'VE ALREADY GOT.

THE BEST WAY TO GAIN SELF-CONFIDENCE IS TO DO WHAT YOU ARE AFRAID TO DO

Tonight it was Josh's turn to put them through their paces. His plan called for more tic tacs, rolls, and single-hand vaults then they'd ever attempted in a single routine, and a cat pass over the final carton that allowed precious little room to stop before the factory wall made contact with your face.

"Are you serious, man?" asked Logan with a grin. "Have you actually tried this?"

"Sure I've tried it. You just have to make sure your hands hit here—" he indicated a spot on the top of the carton "—and not in front of that, or it'll be...a problem."

"No shit," said Logan.

"He's frickin' trying to kill us," said Martin.

Kyle saw Josh's face fall.

"Don't worry, man, it'll be amazing. AMAZING."

While Josh queued up the playlist, Kyle lit a joint and passed it around. "Don't tell Sébastien," he said. Someone made that joke every week. Parkour culture frowns on drugs, but the guys liked the way it lowered their inhibitions, so they pretended they hadn't gotten that memo.

Martin was the last to get the joint. He threw his head back and inhaled deeply, nodding appreciatively as he heard the plaintive opening piano chords of K. Drew's "In Circles" come on:

I've been looking for a way out.
Running around with my head down, my pride in the ground

Then the crashing techno-pop chords at the core of the song came out of nowhere, blasting the pathos of the early measures out of its way:

While they keep running in circles
While they keep running in circles...

Josh cranked up the volume, Martin balanced the joint on a nearby ledge, and one by one they sprinted onto the course, pausing just long enough between departures to keep from getting tangled up later on. With the music throbbing in their ears they leapt between storage containers, vaulted over wooden sawhorses, and somersaulted down concrete ramps, transforming the stark old building into a stage filled with manic, testosterone-fueled motion. In spite of Martin's skepticism everyone executed the routine perfectly, at least until the very end. Kyle's cat pass over the last carton missed the mark Josh had pointed out and the consequences were exactly what Josh had predicted—a problem. He ran hard into the factory wall face-first and fell to the floor on his back just as the music ended, leaving a deafening silence in its wake.

Logan, Martin and Josh ran to the spot where their friend lay motionless on the concrete floor, his eyes closed. No one was sure what to do.

"Do you think he's dead?" Martin asked nervously.

Kyle opened one eye.

"No, I am not fucking dead."

To back up this claim he slowly moved his left foot, then his right knee, then a hand, then an elbow, until he was satisfied that everything was in working order. At first he thought he'd only had the wind knocked out of him, but when he hit the wall he'd actually split his lower lip, and a bright red stream of blood was now inching slowly down his chin toward his white shirt collar. Logan crouched on the floor next to him and used his thumb to push the blood gently back toward Kyle's mouth; then, with a little flip, he took it all away in one large drop. He looked at the scarlet bead on his thumb for a second, then sucked it into his mouth.

"Gross, dude!"

"What are you, a frickin' vampire?"

"Why'd you do that?"

"Dunno. He just looks so...*sexy*, lying there, all vulnerable like. It seemed kind of cool."

"What the fuck, Logan? Are you goin' gay on us?"

Kyle felt a need to weigh in on this possibility.

"If that's the case," he said, sounding a little groggy, "keep your fuckin' hands off me, faggot." Geez, what was this, a goddamn conspiracy today? How had he suddenly become so *appealing* to everyone?

"I didn't think he'd want to get blood on that nice white shirt." Logan gave his thumb one more meditative suck.

"Dude, can you sit up?"

"I think so."

Josh and Martin each took one of Kyle's arms and gently lifted him to a sitting position, resting his back against a carton.

"How does your head feel?"

"OK. I'm just a little shook up, I guess."

"We've all been there."

"I'm really sorry. You guys can go ahead without me."

"No, dude, it's gotta be one for all and all for one. Josh, where'd you leave that joint?"

+   +   +

When Douglas returned home from the Hy-Vee his hands were shaking so badly it took him three tries to get his key inserted in the front door lock. He felt like a turtle with its shell ripped off, exposed for everyone to see. "People will know, they'll know!" he said to himself. "Everybody gossips in this town." He went straight to the medicine cabinet in his bathroom and swallowed an Atavin, hoping it would kick in quickly.

He knew he needed a plan, but as he paced from room to room he couldn't get Gary's angry words out of his head. *Guys like you...* It had never occurred to Douglas that he represented a category of human beings. He wasn't sure what that category was and he didn't want to speculate. *Sick behavior...* Was that true? Was the letter he wrote "sick"? Douglas had no friend to call for perspective. *It's on the security camera tapes...* the man had said. That meant there was film of him leaving the letter under Kyle's register! What would happen when the manager saw that? Would he send the police to Douglas's house?

Thirty minutes later the Atavin was not showing any signs of kicking in, so Douglas went to the bathroom and took another one. His hands continued to shake, making him slosh some water onto the floor when he washed the pill down. He thought of calling his doctor to see if she could prescribe something stronger, but then he'd have to explain why he was feeling so anxious, and he didn't want to do that. The manager had mentioned a sex offender list. Was that something that got printed in the newspaper? Douglas didn't know if he could survive that. Then he remembered the man said that would happen only if he came back to the Hy-Vee, so maybe if he stayed away everything would be all right. But no, nothing would be all right, ever again.

Douglas went to his room and sat at his desk. Maybe he could move away, he thought. He could call a realtor and sell the house. His job could be done from anywhere, after all. But where would he go? His mother had a sister in Kansas, but he barely knew her, and he hadn't seen his cousins since they were children. His whole life had been lived in this town, in this room. The thought of leaving it made him anxious all over again, so he went to the bathroom and took another pill.

It occurred to him that a good movie might calm him down. He had a vast collection recorded on VHS Tapes that filled two bookcases in his room. He pulled *The Crimson Pirate* from the Action and Adventure shelf and popped it in the VCR. The tape continued from where he'd left off the last time. A brilliantly blond Burt Lancaster and his swarthy little sidekick Nick Cravat were getting the best of the Baron Gruda's soldiers as they fought chaotically for control of the pirate ship. Who was that actor playing Baron Gruda? Douglas knitted his brow and peered closely into the TV screen. This was his all-time favorite movie, and he knew every cast member's name by heart. Why couldn't he think of it? Maybe he'd taken too many pills. He'd have to go back to the medicine chest to read the warning label on the Atavin. This time the short journey turned out to be more difficult. After only a few steps Douglas stumbled and fell, hitting his head against the sharp corner of the dresser on the way down. He pushed himself onto his knees and felt his forehead. His hand came away bloody, but he felt no pain. That was odd. He would do something about it when he got to the bathroom to—what was he going to the bathroom for? He'd forgotten. He got to his feet slowly and lurched down the hall anyway. He collected the bottle of Atavin from the medicine cabinet, grabbed a few Kleenex to wipe the blood off his forehead, and went back to his room.

The baron's soldiers had just pushed Nick Cravat overboard, but a cutaway shot revealed that a conveniently protruding cannon had broken his fall and kept him from plunging into the ocean. As he sat astride its barrel he reached one arm back over his head, confident that Burt would rescue him without any call for help. And so he did, whisking the smaller man gracefully onto the deck with a single strong pull. Douglas thought how much he would like to sweep—what was his name, that cashier at the grocery store?—from danger to safety like that. The name just wouldn't come, but the image filled him with contentment. He was feeling calmer at last.

As the room grew darker the lurid hues of 1950s Technicolor washed over Douglas's pale, doughy face and made him one with his childhood. He looked down at his hands; the Atavin looked like the Good & Plenty he'd always chosen when his parents took him to see a movie. Absent-mindedly, he began popping the candies into his mouth, one after another, until he'd eaten them all up.

+   +   +

In spite of Kyle's protests the guys decided their session was over for the night. They drove to the Kum & Go and sent Logan in to get the beer, since he was the only one who was twenty-one. Logan was happy to oblige, because for weeks he'd been working up to asking the clerk who was on duty that night for a date. She seemed really nice but he couldn't figure out whether she was being flirty or just friendly. Tonight he decided to find out.

"Hi, Samantha," Logan said, using his best impression of jaunty. "How are you tonight?"

Samantha was startled by the sound of her name until she remembered her badge.

"Fine, thanks. You?"

"Great! Just need to get some beer. I'll be right back with it."

"OK." Samantha wasn't sure why this guy needed to announce what he was going to buy, but, whatever. She just hoped he wasn't planning to ask her out, like half the guys who came in.

Logan returned with a twelve-pack of Corona.

"ID, please."

"Absolutely."

Logan realized he was introducing himself, in a fashion, and thought Samantha might comment on his name, maybe say "Cool name, Logan!" Instead, Samantha gave the license a perfunctory glance before handing it back and punching a birth date of 1949 into the cash register.

"So, I'm really glad you're here tonight..."

Samantha looked at Logan warily, but he didn't notice.

"Cuz I've been meaning to ask you..."

Samantha rolled her eyes, but Logan plowed on, looking in the general direction of the hot dog oven.

"...whether you might want to go out with me sometime?"

Samantha tapped the credit card terminal impatiently, indicating that Logan should sign.

"Um, that's really nice of you, but no, thanks."

Logan scratched his name across the screen as nonchalantly as possible, but he could feel the heat rising in his face. He made a mental note of the other convenience stores in town he would patronize in the future.

"But you could introduce me to your friend," Samantha added, looking over Logan's shoulder.

"My…"

Logan looked around and saw Kyle perusing the chip rack.

"Him?"

Samantha nodded as she continued to stare in Kyle's direction. Josh and Martin had come into the store to see what the delay was and maybe find a snack to go with the beer, like Twinkies.

Logan's first inclination was to say *I certainly will not introduce you to my friend after you just humiliated me,* but that seemed a little dramatic even to him, so he just said "Kyle, c'mere."

Kyle pulled a bag of sour cream 'n' chives chips off the rack and brought it to the counter. He seemed unaware of Samantha.

"What's up? Do you need money?"

"No, there's someone who would like to meet you."

Kyle turned and looked around the store but saw only Josh and Martin. Logan placed his hands on Kyle's shoulders and rotated him back to face Samantha.

"Samantha, this space cadet is Kyle. Kyle, Samantha."

"Hi, Kyle!"

Kyle took note of the young woman behind the cash register for the first time. She was totally hot, with dark brown hair hanging straight past her shoulders, smooth skin that was remarkably tan for Iowa in early April, and green eyes that had a slightly wicked glint to them. She was definitely out of Kyle's league.

"Um, hi."

"I'm Samantha. I've seen you in the store a couple of times."

"You have?"

Kyle didn't understand why she was talking to him.

"Uh-huh. I think you're pretty cute. Do you have a girlfriend?"

Logan made a scoffing noise and walked away.

"Uh...no, no I don't."

"How is that possible, I wonder?"

Samantha rocked coyly back and forth on her heels.

"Um...I don't...know?"

Kyle's voice went up at the end of the sentence, he had no idea why. He sounded idiotic.

"Ahh, look! You hurt your lip, didn't you?"

She reached across the counter and gently drew her finger across Kyle's broken lip. He shuddered.

"Want me to make it all better?"

"Um..."

Taking that as a yes, Samantha leaned forward, took Kyle's head in her hands and planted a long kiss on his lips, taking care not to press too hard because of his wound. Kyle opened his eyes in surprise, then closed them again as the kiss continued. He had no idea why this was happening, but decided it couldn't hurt to kiss back. It felt pretty good, and Samantha's mint-flavored lip gloss was oddly stimulating.

Josh slapped Martin on the arm and pointed toward the counter. Logan followed his gesture and the three of them looked on in amazement at the PG-13 drama unfolding in front of them.

"Wow," Samantha said as she finally pulled her face away from Kyle's. "That was great!"

Kyle fully agreed, but found himself incapable of more than a slightly goofy smile. Samantha took one of his hands and turned it palm up. Then she took a marker from a cup of pens on the counter and wrote her name and number on his skin.

"Nice hands, too," she said meditatively. She finished writing and let go of Kyle's hand, which fell limply to the counter before he remembered to retrieve it.

"Text me real soon, OK?"

A group of bikers roared into the parking lot, shattering the moment. Kyle looked down at his palm and then back at Samantha. He wanted to make sure she didn't look crazy. She didn't. Just sweet. And very pretty.

"I will," he said quietly. He took the bag of chips without paying for it and walked out to the car, oblivious to his friends in the snack aisle. Josh and Martin stuffed their Twinkies back on the shelf and ran after him. Logan followed with the beer, pointedly not looking in Samantha's direction.

"What the fuck was that?" Logan asked when they were back in the car.

"I know," said Kyle dreamily. He put the key in the ignition but didn't turn it.

"No, I mean what the fuck were you thinking? You knew I wanted to ask her out."

"No, I didn't," Kyle said, surprised out of his stupor. He looked at Logan in the rear view mirror. "You never said..."

"I'm sure I did. Thanks for rubbing my face in it."

"But I didn't know what she was going to do!"

"C'mon, Logan, give him a break," said Martin. "It wasn't Kyle's fault. And, let's face it, you couldn't resist him, either. OW!"

Martin rubbed his bicep where Logan had punched it, smarting at the pain.

"That felt good. Thanks for being there, Martin."

"You're welcome, asshole."

His small act of violence seemed to snap Logan out of his sulk.

"Let's go, lover boy!" he said.

Kyle drove them to North Park, their usual spot, where picnic benches were scattered around the perimeter of a softball diamond. It wasn't really warm enough to sit outside, but since they all lived at home it was better than dealing with nosy siblings and reminders of chores. No sooner had they gotten settled at a table and passed the beer around than the park lights shut off in unison, leaving their bodies silhouetted against the starry sky.

"Man, is it 11:00 already? I've got the early shift in the morning."

Martin was a pipe layer for Reding's Gravel and Excavating, a job he'd trained for right out of high school.

"One lousy bag of potato chips? Is that all we got?" asked Josh. He now regretted leaving the Twinkies on the shelf.

"Technically, they're my chips," said Kyle, "but you're welcome to them."

"Technically, you didn't pay for those chips, so they're stolen merchandise. We better eat 'em before the cops get here."

"Oh, you're right!" Kyle said with a giggle. "I guess I didn't."

"Can't imagine what made it slip your mind," Logan said, sounding bitter again.

"Logan, for Christ's sake, give it a rest. She probably wouldn't have gone out with you anyway."

Logan, sadly acknowledging the truth of this statement, remained silent. Josh picked up the slack.

"So where do you think we'll all be in five years?" he asked.

"You mean, assuming we haven't killed ourselves with parkour?" Martin slapped Kyle gently on the arm with the back of his hand. "You really scared us tonight, man."

"Yeah, sorry."

"Back to my question, gentlemen, please?"

"I'm pretty sure I'll still be laying pipe. Can't beat union benefits."

"And I'll still be trying to finish high school," Josh said with a laugh. He'd developed a bad case of mono his senior year and still hadn't gotten around to making up the credits. He stocked shelves at the K-Mart in the meantime.

"And I will have my degree in hotel management from Cornell and be running a resort in the Canary Islands."

"Loser!"

"And after that I'll look for a job in Europe. Or maybe Buenos Aires."

"Loser!"

"Stop saying that!"

Logan had already gotten an associate's degree in hotel management from Iowa Lakes and put his application in to Cornell.

"Yeah, Josh, can it. If you don't get your act together you'll still be arranging ladies' nylons at K-Mart."

"I *like* ladies' nylons. They're *sexy*."

"Only with ladies *in them*, Josh. Rubbing empty ones over your face doesn't count."

"Do you do that, man? What a perv."

"No, I don't do that. Let's change the subject. Kyle, what about you? Where do you want to be in five years?"

Kyle sat quietly in the darkness as though he hadn't heard the question.

"Hey, earth to Kyle! Is this a slow-growing concussion or something?"

Kyle leaned in toward his friends as though he was about to share a confidence.

"I'm going to make a movie," he said, so softly they couldn't be sure they'd heard him right."

"A *movie?*"

"What the fuck?"

"What about?"

"Parkour."

"Um, I think that's been done. Hello? 'Jump London?'"

"It's going to be called 'Jump Saint Louis.'"

"Why Saint Louis, for God's sake?"

"It has interesting buildings. Parks, architecture. And it's got the Arch. No one would come to see 'Jump Des Moines.'"

"Can I be in it?" asked Martin.

"No."

"Why the fuck not? I'm as good as you."

"Because I want the movie to be about kids who have no confidence in themselves. I want to show them they can become whatever they want."

"How long have you been thinking about this?"

"I thought of it just now."

The group sat in silence, wondering who had taken the cashier from Hy-Vee from their midst and left this visionary.

Kyle looked at the stars. For the first time in his life, he found them looking back at him, beaming down love and encouragement. *You are precious to us*, they seemed to say. How had he never noticed that before? Was this why people thought God was in the sky?

The thought of God made Kyle remember the letter. It had freaked him out at first, but now it seemed like some kind of prophecy. It was as though everyone around him knew what it said and agreed with it: first Marie, then Logan, then

Samantha, and now the stars. He wanted to go home and think about what it all meant.

Martin noticed that Kyle hadn't touched his beer.

"Hey, dude, what's wrong? How come you're not drinkin'?"

Kyle gave his head a little shake.

"I'm good, I'm good. Just not in the mood tonight, I guess."

Martin laid his hand on Kyle's forehead. Kyle liked the way it felt there, warm and reassuring. He could now add Martin to the list of his admirers.

"You coming down with something?"

"No, I'm fine."

He laid his hand on top of Martin's for a brief moment, then gently pushed it off his forehead. He smiled at his friend in the darkness.

"Thanks, man. My ass is getting pretty cold sitting here, though. You guys ready to go?"

Josh snorted.

"Well, we certainly wouldn't want that sweet little ass of yours to feel any pain, would we?"

Josh, too? Wow. Three for three.

It was midnight by the time Kyle had dropped his friends off and parked his car in the garage. He took his shoes off in the laundry room so he wouldn't wake anyone, but when he came into the family room his mother was sitting on the couch reading a book, a glass of white wine beside her. She looked up and smiled as Kyle came in.

"Hi, honey. Did you have a good time?"

"Yeah, Mom." He hoped she wouldn't notice his lip in the soft light of the one lamp. "You're up late."

"I've got exams next week, so I've been cramming. About eleven I decided I couldn't stand one more paragraph of legalese, so I'm clearing my mind with this trash." She waved her book in his direction, and he caught a glimpse of a woman in an eighteenth-century dress being backed against a wall by a man wearing a three-cornered hat.

"Have fun," he said. "I'll see you in the morning."

"OK, good night."

Kyle was almost to the kitchen when his mother spoke again.

"Honey? Did you do something different with your hair?"

Kyle smiled to himself.

"No," he said, turning in her direction. "I don't think so. Why?"

"You just look nice, that's all."

"Thanks, Mom. Good night."

When Kyle got to his room he locked the door and made a beeline for the wastebasket. He fished the letter out and laid it on the desk, smoothing out the wrinkles as best he could. It was his day off tomorrow; he would take the letter to the laundry room and iron it on the back with just a little steam to make it look new again. He examined it closely. For the first time he realized that it had been written by hand; the writing was so neat and elegant that he'd assumed it was some fancy software font. That made it seem all the stranger, since he was sure that no one among his friends or family could pull that off. Who would invest so much time in making this for him? Who cared so much about him?

God?

It was crazy, but nothing else made sense. Kyle hadn't been to church since Benjamin's baptism, and never thought about religion or the Bible at all. He seemed an unlikely candidate to get God's attention. But there was the salutation on the letter: *Dear Kyle*. Wait, though—if it really was from God, did that mean God was gay? Or a woman? Kyle didn't want to think about either of those possibilities. He decided to quit speculating about the author and turn to the nice things the letter had to say about him. He read the phrases over and over, half aloud, until the beauty of their rhythms had taken up lodging in his brain. He crossed the room to his dresser and leaned into the mirror, pushing his hair out of the way so he could see his eyes. *Your eyes are the eyes of doves by the rivers of waters, washed with milk and fitly set.* Kyle didn't really know what that meant, but he noticed for the first time how pretty his eyes were. He raised a hand and stroked one of his cheeks. *Your cheeks are as a bed of spices...* Man, that acne had really cleared up! He had thought he'd have to go through life with those little pits and pock marks, but his skin was now smooth and taut over his high cheekbones, free of any blemish. Why had he not known that? It was like seeing himself for the first time. *As sweet flowers your lips like lilies, dropping sweet smelling myrrh.* Was myrrh anything like mint? He could still smell Samantha's lip gloss if he sniffed hard enough. Kyle righted himself and looked at his reflection from the top of his head to his belt buckle. This was the view Samantha would have had of him over the counter. Not bad. Not bad at all. No wonder she was so into him.

He took one finger and stroked his lip the way Samantha had, and shuddered all over again. This time the shudder extended clear down to his groin and made him stiff. It was partly remembering Samantha's kiss and partly thinking about taking all her clothes off and it was partly just seeing how hot he looked in the mirror that made Kyle tremble all over and realize an overwhelming need to get naked. He jerked his belt back and forth to release the buckle and dropped his pants in one smooth movement, then unbuttoned his shirt with a speed he would not have thought possible. When the last button refused to come undone he ripped the shirt apart with a cry of frustration and threw it across the room. He stepped out of the pants piled around his feet and pulled off his sneakers and socks. Pausing for one last glance in the mirror, he admired the way his bulge was pulling his blue bikini briefs away from his flat stomach.

Still shaking with free-floating desire, he lay down on his bed and began to touch himself all over, reciting the words of the letter softly to himself like some kind of erotic mantra.

My hands are as gold rings set with the beryl... Kyle looked at both his hands, happy with the scars of his true art and even happier with the promise of love that Samantha's number had inscribed there. *My belly is as bright ivory overlaid with sapphires...* He ran his hands over the fine reddish-gold hair that covered his abdomen, and squirmed with pleasure as he dipped his forefinger into and out of his navel. *My legs are as pillars of marble, set upon sockets of fine gold...* He stroked the insides of his thighs, well-pleased with the strong muscles parkour had provided him there. *My countenance is as Lebanon, excellent as the cedars.* He was a goddamned *fox*, and he'd never realized it. Shit, it was like he'd been asleep all his life until he got that letter! He absolutely would make "Jump Saint Louis!" He'd be the movie's producer, and director, and star! And it would go viral on the internet, just like "Jump London," and he'd get invited to do the same thing all over the country. He'd be a goddamned *legend* before he was thirty, he knew it! Thinking about that possibility made him even harder, so he slipped off his shorts to give himself some relief. *My mouth is most sweet; yea, I am altogether lovely.*

"I am!" Kyle said aloud, as his hands brought him right to the verge of ecstasy.

"I am!" he said again, even louder.

Then, as the tidal wave of pleasure finally broke upon the shore, lifting his hips right off the bed, Kyle gave a great, delirious shout of "I AM THE ROSE OF SHARON!" before crashing back onto the sheets, exhausted, but happier than he had ever been in his life.

In their rooms, Annie, Christine and Benjamin each opened their eyes at the same moment, startled by the strange new voice that had wakened them.

The Miraculous Mass of St. Jeremy of Portland

Introit

My heart starts racing the minute I put my foot on the first step leading up to the church doors, and I wonder if I can go through with this. Any moment now someone may recognize me, call out "What are you doing here?" What am I going to say? "I want to be in the congregation as the love of my life celebrates his first Mass"? I could never say that out loud, and, anyway, everybody already knows. Well, not everybody who's here today, but everybody who knew the two of us in seminary. I wonder if Jeremy has thought about whether I'll be here, whether he's thought about me at all. It's a big day for him, one he's waited for all his life. I always thought we'd share it more publicly. I thought I'd be his subdeacon at the altar, our vestments gently brushing against each other as I turned a page of the missal or lifted the pall off the chalice. Instead, I'm out here by myself in street clothes, following the crowd through the huge doorways and hoping nobody I know sees me.

The church looks grand. It's the week after Easter, and the altar is still decked out in lilies and hydrangeas. The altar boys are lighting the six enormous candles behind the altar, so tall they have to use ladders to reach the wicks. This was a diocesan parish until the neighborhood changed and the congregation dwindled. The remnant couldn't afford the upkeep, so the Fraternity was happy to take it off the Archdiocese's hands. That's the Priestly Fraternity of Christ, King and Savior, a traditionalist Catholic society dedicated to the perpetuation of the Latin Mass. We're not widely known— I guess I can't really say "we" anymore—but if you were a traditionalist Catholic new to Portland you'd be all over our website, thrilled to see so many opportunities to worship the way God wants us to, the way God taught us until Vatican II fucked it all up. Pardon my French, I mean *devastated the historic liturgy*. Anyway, that's what we—they—do. Find abandoned or about-to-be-abandoned Catholic churches and make 'em look pretty, ready for the proper worship of God. Where does the money come from? You'd be surprised at just how many Catholics hate the *Novus Ordo* Mass, and just how deep their pockets are.

They've given Jeremy Easter Tuesday, a double second class feast, for his first Mass, a huge honor. At the stroke of 11:00 the tower bells start to bong from high above us, a sound that vibrates right in my solar plexus, and the congregation stands and turns toward the rear of the church. Man, there are a lot of people here. Jeremy will be so pleased when he makes his entrance. No, wait...he won't even notice. All he'll see is that altar up ahead of him.

As the bells die out, the schola begins chanting the Introit from the balcony: "*Aqua sapientiae potavit eos, alleluia: firmabitur in illis, et non flectetur, alleluia.*" After so many years of Latin, it might as well be in English for me: He gave them the water of wisdom to drink, alleluia: it shall be made strong in them, and shall not be moved, alleluia.

Over the heads of the congregation I see the clouds of incense rising from the thurible. A gold processional cross wreathed with lilies makes its way down the aisle behind the thurifer, flanked by two torchbearers, their candles perfectly aligned. The canons from our local community come next in their blue capes, followed by higher-ups from the Fraternity. To my surprise, these turn out to be none other than the Vicar General and the Provincial Superior, men I know only as framed pictures on the wall. These guys don't travel to every first Mass, not by a long shot. Geez, Jeremy, you're a frickin' rock star!

Then it's Jeremy, with his deacon and subdeacon holding his gold and white cope open as he walks, his hands clasped in front of his chest in prayer.

He has never looked more beautiful.

Kyrie

You see, I got thrown out of seminary last month. The official letter, handed to me and mailed to my parents, recommended that I leave in order that I not be an *occasion of scandal to the faithful* by *my objectively disordered lifestyle.* Translation: they caught Jeremy and me *in flagrante delicto,* and he promised never to do it again, but I couldn't do that. I loved him too much, even after he told the rector I'd seduced him in a moment of weakness.

And Jeremy was different after that. He wouldn't touch me any more, or let me touch him, and he started giving me these robotic lectures. "There are only two paths in life, Kevin," he'd say, "the wide and the narrow, and only one bears fruit." "Really?" I wanted to say. "Who are you? What have you done with my Jeremy?" But I didn't. I just stared at him, hoping to break him down, daring him to let me see the old Jeremy again. He just stared back, no pity in his eyes.

Jeremy and I had grown up together, both our families traditionalist, and we'd served as altar boys from the time we were able to learn the Latin responses. *"Introibo ad altare Dei,"* the priest would say, and we'd reply *"Ad Deum qui laetificat juventutem meam"* like we knew what we were saying. Eventually, we did, and it was beautiful: I will go to the altar of God, to God who is the joy of my youth. God *was* the joy of our youth, so much that when we were ten we told our parents we wanted to be priests. But as Jeremy stood looking coldly back at me last month I realized it had never really been my idea. I followed Jeremy to seminary because I wanted to be wherever he was, because I was in love with him from the first day I saw him.

The trouble was, Jeremy was never in love with me. He was in love with the Mass, and with Christ really present there. He had, like, a permanent lump in his throat thinking about the day he'd celebrate the mysteries himself, be the instrument of Christ's self-offering on the altar. And how could I compete with that? I think I only landed on his screen because he thought I wanted the same thing. (And because I wasn't bad to look at, though he'd never admit that.) He'd only talk about our "spiritual friendship," but I don't have a lot of "spiritual friends" whose bodies I know every inch of.

Of course, I didn't love Jeremy that way when we were kids, or even during our first years in seminary. It all started during recreation time one day in our third year. We were playing soccer—in our cassocks, of course, just like we did everything else—and somebody kicked the ball out of bounds. Jeremy and I traipsed after it and found it had rolled down the embankment at the edge of the playing field. We started clambering down the slope, picking our steps carefully because the grass was wet, but I ended up tripping on my cassock and tumbling the last few feet. I landed on my back, my head right next to the soccer ball. Jeremy fell exactly the same way—in retrospect, I realized this was probably not an accident—and managed to land right on top of me. Instead of picking himself up, he just stared at me there underneath him, my hair wet with dew, for what seemed like a long time. Then he said, "Look at you," really quietly, and bent his head down and kissed me.

When we came back up with the ball my face was beet red and I was sure everyone would know what had just happened, but no one noticed. From then on the die was cast, and for the next three years we discovered everything there was to know about how our bodies—and for me, at least, our souls—could connect.

And I am not in the least sorry about that.

Gloria

The fact is, the whole seminary was madly in love with him, priests and seminarians alike, though not one of them would have admitted it. But Jeremy chose me, or, at least let me choose him, which earned me the respect of some and the loathing of many. Jeremy had it all: he was brilliant at languages, knew his theology inside out, sang like an angel, and even composed his own music for our occasional sacred concerts. Oh, he also looked like a movie star. With his high cheekbones, slender nose, and dark, brooding eyes that you could fall into if you looked too long, he was a vocation recruiter's dream, a fact the Fraternity took full advantage of in their publicity materials. Jeremy's close-cropped black hair showed off his perfectly-shaped skull, and his slender, athletic frame looked pretty hot in his perfectly tailored cassock. You'd think that when you were so popular and good-looking you'd adopt a Big Man on Campus attitude, you know, "Hail, Fellow,

Well Met," or some such thing, but not Jeremy. He was quiet and pretty serious most of the time. Solemn, you might say, even when we made love. It wasn't that he was stern or unpleasant, he just didn't crack a smile very often.

Except for the time we went fishing at the end of our fourth year, one of the few occasions in our regimented lives we could do whatever we wanted without someone's permission. We drove up to the Finger Lakes and pitched a tent by one that had a good reputation for fish. Sure enough, our first morning I caught a huge striped bass right off the bat and climbed onto a rock to show Jeremy, who was still baiting his line on the shore. "Look what I've got!" I shouted, then promptly slipped off the rock and hit the water with a big splash, setting my catch free. Jeremy laughed so hard I thought he was going to choke, and all that day he pretended he hadn't seen the fish in my hands, even though I knew he had. "What fish?" he'd say, knitting his brows like I was crazy. I loved it because his teasing made me feel close to him, closer even than when we were in bed. It was one of our best days.

But it wasn't the only one. There was the pilgrimage to Lourdes when we held candles and knelt in the dark with a thousand other pilgrims on the saint's feast day and Jeremy quietly took my hand with his free one. He meant no disrespect for Our Lady or Saint Bernadette, I knew, he only wanted to share the experience of reverencing them more deeply with me. Or the day he brought me daffodils when I was in the infirmary with pneumonia because he knew how much I liked them, not caring what anyone might think. Or keeping watch at the Altar of Repose on Holy Thursday, prostrate next to each other on the chapel floor in front of the reserve sacrament, our elbows just touching, participating in Jesus's agony in the garden and our own at not being able to express our love more freely. At least, I think that's what was going through our minds. We didn't talk about our relationship very much...well, at all. We just lived it.

The Mass of the Catechumens is nearly ended. The Vicar General has finished his sermon, not a single word of which I can recall, and we stand as Jeremy intones the first words of the *Credo* and the schola takes it up from there. Soon the Mass of the Faithful will begin. I'm frustrated that I can't see Jeremy better. I had so wanted to stand next to him at this moment. Maybe I still can.

After the Creed I fall to my knees and bow my head like I'm praying in earnest but it's really so I can concentrate, open my second sight, the way we were taught in the Ignatian Exercises on so many retreats. I was always good at it; it just came naturally to me to imagine myself in a scene from the Gospels, walking with Jesus and the disciples on dusty Galilean roads, smelling the acacia trees and hearing the sparrows chirp, being present to the sacred story in every detail. So now I rise up in heart and mind to where Jeremy is, preparing the offering at the altar. *Ascendo.*

I am floating over the heads of the congregation...there's our confrère Roger Kenney, the shit, most likely the Judas who told the rector where he could find Jeremy and me that night and what we would be doing. I'd seen how he looked at Jeremy and how he looked at me, as well. If looks could kill, I wouldn't be here now.

Let it go, Kevin.

There's Jeremy's family in the front pew, his parents and his twin brother and his two sisters and his grandmother, her face lined from the pain of her arthritis. If things hadn't gone the way they'd gone I'd be joining all these people for a festive lunch after the Mass is over. Now I probably won't even get to say hello to them. They still don't know why I left seminary, and I doubt my parents will tell them. If they knew...God, what a mess.

Let it go, Kevin.

Now I'm at the altar, directly behind Jeremy as he prepares the paten and chalice. I'm standing so close that my nose is practically in his hair, which smells faintly of some kind of tonic, something he must have done just for today. It makes me smile to think of him deciding to do something like that. I can see him at the drug store, looking at the options, wondering which one to get. I've never known him to take the slightest interest in toiletries; even his clothes were only protection from immodesty.

He's almost done with the preparations, now. He bends at the waist, supporting himself by placing his hands on the altar. "*Suscipe, sancta Trinitas, hanc oblationem...*" Receive, O Holy Trinity, this oblation... I'm transfixed by the gracefulness of his splayed fingers on the starched white cloth. Then he turns to address the congregation, who stand as one.

"*Orate, fratres,*" he says, extending his hands. Pray, brethren, that my sacrifice and yours may be acceptable to God the Father Almighty. I'm standing so close that I can feel his sweet breath on my face, but, of course, *I'm not really here,* it's just my imagination. So when Jeremy's gaze wavers just the tiniest bit before he turns back to the altar and I'm pretty he sure he's looking *at* me, not *through* me, I nearly collapse to the floor. How is this possible? But it doesn't stop there.

All of a sudden I am not looking at the back of Jeremy's head any more. I am looking at the framed altar cards and the tabernacle and the bleached white corporal, the Host lying on its paten and the ornate silver chalice filled with wine. I have become one with him, seeing what he sees, making every gesture with him. I'm scared out of my wits and I don't know how to undo this.

Offertorium

We turn and face the congregation again.

"*Dominus vobiscum,*" I hear us sing in a clear tenor voice much better than mine.

"*Et cum spiritu tuo,*" the schola sings back, with a few members of the congregation joining in.

"*Sursum corda,*" lift up your hearts, we chant next, then turn back to face the altar.

Now that I'm thinking with him I realize that Jeremy has a *plan,* that he hasn't forgotten about me at all, that I am in fact central to this, his first Mass, but not in a way I like...not one bit. I look down at the Host through Jeremy's eyes and understand that in his mind it's *us*, and he's offering *us* up, letting us go. I want to beg him to stop, but he is relentless.

"*Te igitur, clementissime Pater...benedicas haec dona, haec munera, haec sancta sacrificia illibata.*" We therefore beg of thee, most merciful Father, that thou wouldst bless these gifts, these offerings, these holy and unspotted oblations... Jeremy makes the sign of the cross three times over the bread and wine with his hand held stiffly at an angle, like a blade slicing our last three years into pieces.

Stop it, Jeremy, *stop it*. Don't give what we had away, don't give it back to God...it's ours! Goddamn it, it's *ours*!

But there is no stopping the ineluctable power of the Mass. We've come to its very heart, the words of Jesus at the Last Supper, words now issuing for the first time from the lips of my beloved: Who, on the day before He suffered, took bread into His holy and venerable hands...and gave it to His disciples, saying: 'Take, eat...

"*HOC EST ENIM CORPUS MEUM.*"

The acolyte rings the Sanctus bells raucously to announce the miracle. But I only want to stop it from happening.

No, Jeremy, no! *This* is your body, you are *my* body! Can't you see that? Can't you *see that*? My inner voice is choking back tears but Jeremy's face remains placid, concentrated, rapt. We drop on one knee before the miracle of transubstantiation, rise and elevate the paten above our head, then genuflect once more, a kind of dance of reverence. The subdeacon removes the pall from the top of the chalice.

In like manner...he took the chalice, and gave it to His disciples, saying: 'Take, drink...

"HIC EST ENIM CALIX SANGUINIS MEI."

The bells sound like a fire alarm going off in my brain.

Oh, God, oh God, Jeremy, this cup is *our* blood, we're the ones who are bleeding! All the nights we held each other for dear life, the secret gestures when we passed in the hall that made us closer than our parents ever were, our early morning runs when we would breathe as one, you're pouring them all out and we'll never get them back!

Down again, up again, down once more. Our thumbs and forefingers are pinched together now, sheltered from touching anything else because they have touched the Body and Blood of our Lord.

I take several deep breaths to try and calm myself. With my inner voice silent I can hear the ancient words coming from Jeremy's lips with new attentiveness.

"...panem sanctum vitae aeternae, et calicem salutis perpetuae." The bread of eternal life, and the chalice of endless salvation, he says, making the sign of the Cross over the elements once more. My panic begins to subside. Yes, he's giving us away, but he's also blessing us, saying what we had was holy. Oh God, give me grace to accept this, please. *Please.*

"...jube haec perferri per manus sancti Angeli tui in sublime altare tuum..." Bid these offerings to be brought by the hands of Thy Holy Angel to Thine altar on high... A radiant light

enfolds us as Jeremy's voice continues the prayer, gently yet clearly, and then I can't hear him anymore because the sound of beating wings has drowned it out.

I faint.

Communio

Another ring of the Sanctus bells brings me to myself. I am once again in my pew, on my knees, and the congregation is rising to move forward and take communion. I don't plan to join them. Whatever the hell just happened, it's left me feeling sullen and resentful. Jeremy is taking our love and giving it away in little pieces to hundreds of people, placing it on the tongues of our friends and enemies at seminary, visiting dignitaries and family members, countless people he doesn't even know. It's theirs now, no longer ours, and they won't even know it.

I turn my legs sideways to let the people in my pew brush past me. They probably assume I'm a Protestant, or maybe a Jew. I don't care. I just don't want a tiny piece of something that once belonged to me entirely.

There are a lot of people in the congregation and everyone wants to receive from the new priest, so I have plenty of time to think. Enough that my convictions about Jeremy's betrayal begin to fray around the edges. I mean, what did I think would happen after seminary? The Fraternity sends its priests all over the country, all over the world. We would have been separated anyway, maybe for years at a time. And it's not like we could ever be a *couple*, like those frickin' Episcopalian priests getting married left and right by *their bishops*, for Christ's sake. Those guys are just like the rest of secular society...they're not *set apart*, the way we are, the way Mary and Joseph were. How do they think they could ever offer a valid Mass? Well, of course, they can't anyway, even the ones married to women. Still...the idea that in our country, even in many parts of the world, Jeremy might have become my...No, I can't say it, it's too ridiculous. Jeremy would think so, too. Maybe he did the only thing that really makes sense in our world, and I just didn't have the heart to admit it.

My sullenness is lifting and I realize time is running out for me to have any further contact with Jeremy before the Mass is over and his family and friends whisk him away. I don't want the day to end like this, refusing communion from—*with*—Jeremy. I decide I'll go up for a blessing after the conclusion of the Mass. I try not to think about the fact that this may be the last time Jeremy and I will ever touch. To distract myself, I read the bulletin's information about getting a blessing from a new priest after his first Mass:

> *A plenary indulgence is granted under the usual conditions to a priest on the occasion of a first Mass he celebrates with some solemnity, as well as to the faithful who assist at the Mass. Moreover, a partial indulgence is granted to the faithful who kiss the palms of a newly ordained priest, both on the day of ordination and on the day of a first Mass. These indulgences promote and reward*

personal devotion and manifest honor toward the mystery of the Eucharist and the priesthood. We thank Fr. Jeremy for providing such an opportunity for grace to us today.

Wow! It's practically a Get Out of Jail Free card, a chance to double dip. I want to turn and say this to the woman next to me in the pew but she looks pretty pious so I decide against it. My jocularity is probably just a way of distancing myself from that part about kissing the priest's palms, something I'd sort of forgotten about.

The retiring procession is making its way down the aisle now. I catch a glimpse of Jeremy's radiant face; he's clearly still back there in that place out of time we shared for a few brief moments. It's like there's some kind of force field around him; I can't believe I ever put my lips on his, rubbed them raw with my desire. Now it would seem like some kind of violation.

I make my way forward to the altar rail, following the crowd. In for a penny, in for a pound, my mother always said.

Ite, missa est

As I kneel between people I don't know I come back to my original question: can I go through with this? It may be a partial indulgence for everyone else but for me it's a little different. I've kissed those hands in the middle of the night, grateful for their ministrations of an entirely different sort. I look out of the corner of my eye to see how much contact to expect. I'm dreading the touch of his hands on my scalp because I'm afraid it will be *objective*, symbolic, drained of any history between our bodies, the touch of any new priest on any congregant presenting himself for a blessing.

Oh, God, I'm next already.

I want to pull my head into my shoulders like a turtle, but that'll look ridiculous so I just stare straight ahead as though I don't even know the man who's about to pray God's blessing down upon my objectively disordered self. With a slight swish of linen Jeremy is in front of me, towering over me. I bow my head calmly, trying not to betray any sign of my thumping heart. And then his hands are on me: gentle, firm, and—oh, my dearest God, *thank you*—full of love.

Let me remember this. It's the last time I'll ever feel his hands on me. *Let me remember this.*

"*Benedicat vos omnipotens Deus: Pater, et Filius, et Spiritus Sanctus. Amen.*" The blessing is over before it begins, and Jeremy presents his palms before my face. I try desperately to memorize every line, every crease. Then, with all the tenderness I can muster, I pull them toward my lips and place a kiss on each of them, on the very spot the bishop anointed to inscribe the wounds of Christ, kissing them, and Jeremy, goodbye. "*Tu es sacerdos in aeternum, secundum ordinem Melchizidech.*" Thou art a priest forever, after the order of Melchizidek. You *are*, Jeremy, you are.

I raise my head just as the tears return and start streaming down my cheeks. I'm too worn out to be embarrassed, and too filled with love to feel self-conscious. But I don't want Jeremy to misunderstand. I know he can see my wet face and I don't want him to think I'm pathetic, heartbroken...I want him to understand that I get it now, I finally *get it*, and I am so very happy for him and for the life he's chosen, a life that I never could have sustained, not without him at my side, and that could simply never be. I assume he'll move on to the next parishioner and spare me the stares of the people around me, but he doesn't. With every muscle fiber resisting it I tilt my head up to look at his face, his blessed face, blurry through my tears. I wipe the back of my hand across my eyes and look again, and I see that Jeremy, solemn Jeremy, is *smiling* at me, and it's not pity and it's not superficial but it's every bit as filled with joy as the time I fell into the lake and lost my fish and he laughed until he choked, but it's more than that, better. It's like the Blessed Mother herself, *full of grace*, holding me, cherishing me, telling me I will be alright, God's own love delivered to me by Jeremy, His instrument. I smile back at him shyly, knowing I will never, ever have the opportunity to tell him what has happened to me today. Then, with a small tap on my shoulder, he moves on to the next person.

I will carry that smile with me until the moment I leave this earth.

The Mass is ended. Go in peace.

Snow Day

**The Parish Church and School, Frösön, Sweden
8 March 1842**

August found the darkened church even colder than he'd expected. He winced at the bitter air that struck his face as soon as he swung the heavy wooden door to the bell tower open. How glad he would be to get back to his tiny apartment in the school building, where he'd started a fire in the parlor as soon as he'd risen thirty minutes ago. After a year in Frösön he had yet to acclimate to nine months of winter or the puny allowance he was given for fuel, the bulk of which had to be used to heat the school during the week. Perhaps today he would enjoy the children's heat all by himself.

It had snowed all weekend, adding a foot or more to the two feet already on the ground. School would be closed; he'd be a headmaster with no one to oversee. By ringing the church bell promptly at six, August would alert the villagers to this fact and let them make their lists of tasks for the children to work at about the house. In Stockholm a snow day had always been a play day, but the residents of Frösön were opposed to merriment of any kind. (August considered them Norwegians at heart, despite their now-official allegiance to King Karl Johan.)

He took out his pocket watch and opened it, waiting for the stroke of six. He looked dispassionately at the picture of Liliane, his fiancée, inside the watch's cover. They had known each other since childhood and now at last were to be married in July by mutual agreement of their parents, rather than because of any passion or even attraction between them. But they were dutiful children, and, at least outwardly, pious. "Be fruitful and multiply," August said to himself with little sense of anticipation. "Be fruitful and multiply."

The minute hand slipped onto the twelve and August pulled hard on the bell cord. From high above him a resonant clang pierced the brittle morning air, traveling throughout the island and across the lake to the new town of Östersund. No doubt its inhabitants were scratching their heads and wondering if it might be Sunday after all. But everyone in Frösön would know the meaning of the bell and eye their children appraisingly, wondering just how much they might get done around the house without breaking something.

August hurried back through the church, out a rear door and along the covered walkway that connected the church to the school. The snow swirled furiously across his boots, submerging them briefly and then hurrying on to bury the next thing in its path. August reached out anxiously for the school's back door, regretting his gloveless hands. He stomped his feet on the floor of the mud closet inside and shook the snow from the heavy cloak he'd worn in place of his frock coat.

In his living quarters on the second floor, August lit the stove and cut two slices from yesterday's stale loaf of bread. He laid them in the oven to toast and put the kettle on for tea. He longed for some eggs, but his stingy parishioners gave him only *lutfisk* and *akvavit*, and those only at Christmas. He fetched the jar of orange marmalade that Liliane had sent him from the shelf and spooned a tiny portion onto a plate, hoping to stretch it out as long as possible.

The kettle whistled and he filled the teapot, then knelt on the hardwood floor with his prayer book to say his morning devotions. These were largely meaningless to him, but he recited them out of a sense of duty and to prove that he was not the "young Pharisee" his bishop had summed him up to be, sending him to this frozen outpost to learn humility. He would take his abasement in stride, not set a foot off the straight path, so that the church would eventually say to him "Friend, come up higher." His prayers in that regard, at least, were heartfelt.

His duty rendered, he sat down at the small table near a window opaque with frost and picked up Liliane's most recent letter. It had arrived last Friday but he had not yet opened it. He did so now and perused the gracefully flowing penmanship.

My dearest August,

I hear reports of the continuing bitter weather in Jämtland and worry for your health and safety. It has been sunny in Stockholm and rather mild. The Almstedts' garden is awash in bluebells, a lovely sight. But perhaps it is cruel of me to tell you that when you are surrounded by so much snow. Of course, it won't be long before I see it for myself, assuming the bishop does not relent and give you another appointment some place warmer.

Mama insists that I accompany her to the dressmaker's tomorrow to choose my wedding gown. As you well know, such things have never interested me, but Mama is tremendously excited. I'll be sure to act suitably enthusiastic about whichever dress she likes the best.

Please tell me whether or not you like orange marmalade. I'm not entirely sure you do and can always make something else.

Your affectionate Liliane

August laid the letter on the table and contemplated a lifetime of such inanities at every meal. It was not that he despised or even disliked Liliane; he had simply found no one else whose company he preferred. Of course, he had not really looked, either.

When he had finished his breakfast he washed the dishes and put some more wood on the fire, fully intending to indulge himself with the heat not needed elsewhere in the building. He passed the pier glass between the parlor's windows and noted that his moustache had become unruly. Retrieving a small pair of scissors from the dresser in the bedroom, he set about trimming it.

August would be twenty-nine years old in May, but looked considerably younger. It was for that very reason he had grown the moustache, but he maintained it with military precision, not willing to follow the herd on excessively bushy beards and mutton-chop sideburns. His reddish-blond hair was kept neatly trimmed by weekly visits to the village barber, and his blandly pleasant features charmed the ladies without posing any threat. Only his eyes contradicted the placidness of his overall appearance; large and round, they seemed to question everything in the world around them even as their owner recited his platitudes from the pulpit.

As the morning wore on the snow finally ceased to fall, and shortly before noon August's three faculty members arrived to help him shovel out the path to the school door, a rather pointless endeavor given the impassability of the roads. The young men respected their headmaster and recognized his superior education and upbringing. They had each brought something for a luncheon meal, which the men enjoyed together at three, as the sun was already declining.

After the teachers had returned home August locked the school's front and back doors and wandered through the classrooms, taking stock of the various demonstrations that numbers and letters and the Swedish language and history were being duly acquired. A final ray of red-orange light broke through a heavy cloud bank and bathed the stark white walls in its glow for a brief moment before the clouds engulfed it once more. As though taking the darkness as its cue, the snow resumed at once, falling thick and wet, seemingly determined to wipe out the afternoon's work.

August contemplated how we would spend the rest of the day. He had already written his sermon for the following Sunday, a plea for sobriety that would no doubt rankle at least half the men in his congregation but had to be made for the sake of the children. There was a shelf of rather good fiction in the library; perhaps he would begin a novel. He lit an oil lamp and began to climb the stairs.

On the third step he was startled to hear the sound of the piano being played in the music room. The building was completely silent yet the notes were muffled, as though the door to the room had been closed. Had one of the teachers remained behind? Why wouldn't he have just said so? Could a child have stowed away in the school overnight? But no, the playing was too expert. He recognized the piece, a mazurka of Monsieur Chopin, whom he had heard play a rare concert in Paris years earlier. August continued to climb the stairs, perplexed and more than a bit disturbed by this strange turn of events. He crossed the landing and put his hand on the knob of the music room door, wondering if he should perhaps flee instead.

He turned the knob and the door creaked open, insulting the beauty of the music. At the piano sat a young man of sixteen or seventeen whom August had never seen before. He was dressed elegantly in a black frock coat and dove-colored pants and waistcoat, with a black cravat wound around a high white collar of a sort that had not been fashionable for over a decade. It did not seem possible that he was from Frösön, dressed in such a way. The young man did not look up when August entered, nor did he cease the mazurka.

August looked about the room and saw that it was lighted by multiple kerosene lamps casting a comforting yellow glow. He didn't recognize some of the lamps and wondered where they had come from. He turned again to the young pianist. A mass of light brown curls framed his epicene features and cascaded over the back of his collar. His eyes were cast down to the keyboard, splaying his long lashes over the pale skin beneath them. He held his slender body erect as his graceful hands moved calmly but masterfully over the keys.

August felt powerless to interrupt the flow of the music, and so he waited until the piece came to its conclusion. The young man held his hands over the keyboard as the echo of the last notes passed into silence, then rested them in his lap. August cleared his throat, struggling to find his voice.

"Who...who are you? How did you get in here?"

The young man raised his eyes for the first time and looked directly at August, who took a step backwards in consternation. Why was this stranger looking at him like that, as though he knew him?

"Answer me! How did you get in here?"

The young man said nothing as he continued to regard August calmly.

Seized by a sudden thought, August ran out of the room and down the stairs, taking them two at a time. He pulled back the bolt of the front door and threw it open. The snow whipped at his face and stung his eyes, but at last he was able to make out that there were no footprints on the white ground, already as smooth as before he and the teachers had dug a pathway. He slammed the door and ran to the other one, where he found the same thing.

The music resumed, another mazurka.

August climbed slowly back to the music room, not knowing what else to do. This time he did not mind interrupting the music.

"I say, this is insufferable. Tell me who you are and how you got into my school. I am the headmaster, Pastor Holgersson."

The young man ceased playing when August began to speak and again turned his face calmly in the older man's direction.

"I know who you are, August."

August shuddered at the sound of his name.

"How...how do you know my name?"

The young man smiled to himself and began playing again, an impromptu this time.

August felt a foreign urge to burst into tears without knowing why. The music seemed to be speaking to his secret vulnerability, coaxing it into the open like a frightened animal. The notes penetrated his solar plexus and flew merrily up his spine to his brain, where they exploded in bursts of color. Was this what intoxication felt like? August had never been drunk.

His alarm and anger were lessening now, and he found himself walking toward the piano, putting one foot ahead of the other in a kind of trance. He was beginning to understand that the laconic young man was using the music to converse with him, and, recognizing this, August listened all the more keenly. He saw fields of mountain flowers blowing in a southerly wind, their hues riotous under the springtime sun. Next came waterfalls tumbling into fjords with inexhaustible force, then the serene interior of an empty church, golden rays falling diagonally from the clerestory windows onto the stone floor below.

August had reached the piano. "May I sit next to you?"

The young man nodded his head almost imperceptibly as he continued the impromptu.

August sat down on the long bench, leaving only a tiny aperture between his hip and the pianist's. He became intensely aware of the young man's physical presence—the supple folds in the sleeves of his frock coat, the small puffs of breath emanating from his handsome nose, a faint scent of bergamot radiating from somewhere inside his dress. It seemed he had never really noticed another human being in such vivid detail before; why was that? He became fascinated by the motion of the young man's slim leg as it moved up and down on the pedals. With some effort he turned from that sight to gaze at the young man's head; why weren't either of them more self-conscious, he wondered? August doubted that he had ever been this close to another human being. On an impulse he brushed the curls away from the young man's ear and tenderly kissed it. The young man played on, unperturbed, though a faint smile spread once more across his lips.

"You liked that? Do you want me to do it again?" August had never kissed anyone before.

"If you like."

August kissed the ear a second time, then the cheek. "Won't you tell me your name now?" he asked sweetly.

The young man stopped playing and turned toward August, their faces close enough to feel each other's breath.

"I am your desire, August."

"My..." August recoiled in horror from the mysterious visitor. He leapt to his feet. "My *desire*? How dare you say such a thing? How dare you?"

The young man held his gaze, offering no defense and no further interpretation of his words. He turned back to the piano and began playing again.

"Stop that! Stop playing that piano!"

But the young man did not stop, so August lunged toward him and slapped his face with such force that he began to bleed from his cheek and nose. The pianist shook his head as though to clear it, then resumed his playing. The motion scattered scarlet drops across the glistening white keyboard, a sight which momentarily transfixed August, who had neither kissed nor struck anyone before. He was desperate to make the young man leave.

"Explain yourself! What do you mean by saying you are my desire? You're obviously a human being like myself! Certainly, you bleed like one. But you're a human being I've never laid eyes upon before this day, so how could you possibly know anything about me?" August had come to accept that nothing he said would stop the flow of music filling the room, so he merely shouted over it. "I have no desire! I have only duty! A duty to my parishioners, a duty to marry Liliane! And that is as it should be, because the ranks of hell are filled with those who cared only about their desire!"

August staggered about the room, feeling like a caged animal. For a final time he planted his feet and addressed the young man with all his force.

"Do you hear?" he screamed. "I have no desire!"

He rushed toward the young man and glared at him with all the fierceness he could command. The music stopped for a moment and the pianist looked up at August expectantly.

"I have no desire," he muttered miserably, then took the young man's face in his hands, and pressed his mouth violently upon the other's.

When August finally pulled back with a cry of self-loathing, the visitor no longer looked benign. He returned to his music with even greater intensity, a ballade in a minor key that demanded a forceful attack of the keyboard. Gone were the visions of flowers and waterfalls from August's mind, replaced by scenes of souls writhing in agony amid the flames of hell. He ran from the room, inchoate moans of despair arising from deep in his throat.

He ran down the stairs once more, but this time he stumbled and fell the last length, collapsing in a heap at the bottom. The music still swirled about him, sounding as close now as it had in the room above. He had to get away from it, had to make it stop. He leapt to his feet and threw open the front door once more. In spite of the fact that he was dressed only in shirt sleeves he ran out into the frigid night and was engulfed at once in the whirling, biting snow. Using all his strength he lifted one foot after the other, making his way as best he could away from the school and the music.

After a hundred yards the music was as loud in his ears as ever, after two hundred yards the same. His fate had become clear to him. Which direction was the lake? He had to get to the lake. For now he knew with certainty that it would be only there, deep beneath its icy waters, that the terrible music would finally be silenced.

Boys of the World, Unite!

Pathé News, June 4, 1935: The French liner Normandie completed its maiden voyage in record time today, sailing from Le Havre to New York in 4 days, 3 hours and 14 minutes. In anticipation of this accomplishment commemorative silver medallions were minted in advance of the ship's departure and distributed to all its 2,000 passengers. Among these were Madame Albert Lebrun, wife of the president of France, and fifteen-year-old Roger Charbonneau, "ambassador" from the boys of France to the Boys' Clubs of America. A young New Yorker, Peter Blakelee, will return with M. Charbonneau in a week's time and represent the Boys' Clubs to France.

Charles's collar felt too tight. He slipped a finger under it to see if he could make it a little roomier, then found he couldn't get it back out. Worried that someone would notice his predicament and laugh, he gave a great yank upward, freeing his finger but scratching his face with his thumbnail. A fine red line raised itself immediately, looking very much like a fencing scar. It was going to be that kind of morning, he could tell.

He couldn't remember why he'd been chosen to be the official representative of the Boys' Club of New York to greet the young "ambassador" being sent from their French counterpart in Paris. Charles always got red in the face when asked to speak in public, and he had a stammer to boot. Why hadn't they just asked Peter? He even spoke French, which was why he was going to be the Club's representative over there.

Charles's tie kept going crooked no matter how many times he straightened it. His suit was new for the occasion, stiff and confining. He looked down at his notes for the fortieth time. The sweat stains on the index card had begun to turn the ink in their vicinity into blue blotches. Panicked that he might have to improvise, Charles held the card gingerly between his thumb and forefinger and shook it in the air, hoping it would dry by the time he needed it.

Just then the *Normandie* sounded its great horn, signaling that the passengers were about to disembark. Startled by its loudness, Charles lost hold of his notes. He watched them sail gaily through the air on the light June breeze and drop into the Hudson River, where they were soon indistinguishable from the colorful debris already floating there.

What had been written on that card?

In spite of having read it over and over again, Charles's mind was a blank. His panic increasing by the moment, he tried desperately to picture the card and its precious helps to his poor memory. "Sincere welcome..." "happy relationship..." "on behalf of the Boys' Club of New York..." That was about all he could come up with, and it wasn't nearly enough.

The Club administrator had cabled the "ambassador," whose name was Roger Charbonneau, and told him to look for a banner that said *The Boys' Club of New York Welcomes You* somewhere near the bottom of the gangway. He had also given notice to the principal newspapers to ensure there would be coverage of the arrival.

The first-class passengers, including the French president's wife, had made their way off the ship, and Roger had traveled second, so he might be here any moment. Charles was torn between trying to outline a new speech and just winging it. His upper lip began to sweat.

"Look! There he is!" said Mrs. Carpenter, the chairwoman of the Boys' Club board and the organizer of the exchange. She pointed to a nattily dressed young man halfway down the gangway who was waving in the group's direction, having spied the promised welcome banner. With no time left, Charles would have to wing it.

Roger had nearly reached the welcoming committee when he realized he was being photographed by the press. He retreated a few steps up the gangplank for a better sight line and struck a pose, pushing his jacket aside to place a hand on one hip. Charles had never seen anyone like him. The pants of Roger's light grey suit were elaborate plus-fours, their elegant drape falling softly over bold argyle knee socks that descended into lace-up brown Oxfords of an unusually graceful style. His pale lavender tie was wide and expensive-looking and had what looked to be an amethyst stick pin inserted in it. A white handkerchief lined in purple exploded out of his breast pocket, completing the effect of...well, Charles wasn't sure just what to call it, but it certainly made an impression. As did Roger's fine head, like that of a young French movie star, with high cheekbones, a strong Roman nose and lively brown eyes, all topped by a rakish shock of wavy chestnut hair.

Charles's mouth felt dry.

From his perch on the gangway Roger looked down at Charles, squinting up at him in the sun, and liked what he saw: an all-American in his mid-teens: blond, blue-eyed and freckled, tall for his age and slender, just like in the magazines.

I am going to eat this boy for the little lunch, he told himself, in what he thought was impeccable English.

"Thanks, son," a newsman called. "Can we get a couple of you greeting your hosts?"

"But of course," Roger replied. He stepped off the gangway and crossed to the welcome banner in a few long strides. He looked from one face to another, waiting to see who would speak first. Everyone turned to Charles, who was struggling to get the lump out of his throat. At last he stepped forward and offered Roger his hand. The flash bulbs exploded.

"B...b...bee-en-venoo," he began, exhausting his knowledge of French at one blow. "Welcome to the United States." Up close Roger was several inches shorter than Charles, but the aura of confidence that surrounded him made any such difference negligible. He did not so much shake

Charles's hand as place his own palm down inside it, as though he expected Charles to kiss it.

"My name is Charles, Charles Whitehead, and I'm the president of the Boys' Club of New York."

Oh, of course! *That's* why he'd been asked to do this.

"Vehry good, zank you," said Roger, flashing a brilliant smile at the whole group but mostly at Charles, who blushed. "I am vehry happy to be here."

Charles's face went blank for a moment as he prayed for the next line of his prepared remarks to float to the surface; he hoped it wouldn't be obvious in the pictures. All at once he remembered it, just as the photographers resumed shooting.

"Our two countries have a long history of a happy relationship with one another, and we look forward to cementing that relationship further by these mutual visits."

Roger knit his brows, unsure of the meaning of the word "cementing." What, exactly, was this charming boy wishing for him?

"We hope that you will enjoy the sights and experiences we have planned for your visit, and that you when you return to France you will have many new American friends." Charles felt better, getting this part out. If only he could remember the last thing...

"The *cap*," hissed Mrs. Damrau, the club's matron.

"Oh," said Charles, and retrieved the Yankees cap he'd apparently dropped. He dusted it off and handed it to Roger.

"A little welcome gift," he said, relieved to be quit of his duties.

"Zank you," said Roger, looking at the cap suspiciously. He held the cap up to the photographers and smiled. They took their final pictures and went to find the First Lady of France, who was being greeted by a committee of the American Red Cross.

"Aren't you going to put it on?" asked Mr. Morgan, the athletic director.

Roger was fiercely protective of his hair.

"Of course," he said vaguely, "all at the hour."

The welcoming committee looked at one another, confused.

"*Tout à l'heure,* in a moment, of course!" Peter volunteered, thrusting a hand in Roger's direction. "*Je m'appelle Peter Blakelee, Roger. Je vais rentrer avec vous en quelques jours.*"

Roger shook Peter's hand limply, unimpressed by the sound of his native tongue.

"*Vous parlez le français assez bien,*" he said primly, to Peter's chagrin.

The remaining members of the committee introduced themselves and added their own messages of welcome. Roger was relieved that no further souvenirs of New York were included.

"My *bagages,* where will they be found?" he asked Mr. Morgan, a bit imperiously.

"Your luggage? How much do you have?"

Roger seemed to be counting in his head.

"A, how do you say, *steamer trunk*...and...*un, deux, trois valises*. Three small cases."

Mr. Morgan looked flabbergasted.

"But you're only here for three days!" he blurted out.

"Yes?"

Roger stared impassively at Mr. Morgan, waiting for the desired answer.

"I'll get a porter," muttered the athletic director, shuffling off into the crowd.

"Vehry good," Roger said.

The committee began to make its way to the waiting cars. Roger looped his arm through Charles's as they brought up the rear of the little procession. Charles looked down at their linked elbows in stupefaction.

"Uh..."

"We shall be great friends, yes? How do you say? Buddies of the breast!"

"Oh," was all Charles could think to say.

There wasn't enough room in the cars they'd come in to get Roger and his luggage back to the Avenue A Clubhouse, so a taxi had to be hired. Roger quickly claimed it for himself—and Charles.

"Charles and I will ride in the *tac-see*, OK? You know the way, yes?" he added to his new companion.

"Yes," replied Charles, sounding a bit nervous.

"OK, then, *on y va!*" said Roger, climbing into the cab. Charles looked at Mr. Morgan pleadingly, hoping he'd get in, too; surely they wouldn't let the two teens take the cab on their own! But Mr. Morgan had already soured on Roger, so he returned to his colleagues.

"Good luck," Charles heard him say as he walked away.

"116 Tenth Avenue," Charles told the driver after he'd slid in beside Roger and closed the door.

Whatever hesitation Charles had felt about sharing a taxi with Roger soon evaporated when the young Frenchman turned all his attention to the view outside the window as they made their way down the west side of Manhattan. It was hardly the most scenic introduction to the city, but Roger seemed to love it. He marveled at the enormity of the Empire State Building and strained at the window to look south along the crowded waterfront.

"What are you looking for?" Charles asked.

"I am trying to see again the statue."

"The Statue of Liberty?"

"*La Liberté éclairant le monde,*" he murmured reverently. "It is we who gave it to you."

"Yes," said Charles. "Thank you."

Roger turned to look out the rear window for another glimpse of the Empire State Building.

"*C'est formidable.* Even in Paris we have nothing like this."

"Nobody does, actually," said Charles, hoping that didn't sound boastful.

The skyscraper was lost from sight now, and Roger turned to look at Charles's profile.

"But, what is *thees?*"

He ran a thumb tenderly over the red scar on Charles's cheek.

Charles shuddered.

"You did this with an *épeé*, perhaps?"

"I don't know what that is."

He wanted to reach up and push Roger's hand away but it seemed rude.

"It's a—*comment dit-on?*—a kind of sword, very thin, for the...the.. *fen-seeng.*"

"I did it with my thumb," Charles said, feeling foolish.

"I have with me some cream, it will make it feel better."

"OK," said Charles, wondering if Roger planned to apply it himself. Probably.

They had arrived at the Clubhouse, where photographers for the Boys' Clubs of America were poised and ready. After all, this French kid was going to meet Al Smith, the four-term governor of New York, this afternoon, and President Roosevelt later in the week. Their publicity department would go ape over this.

Roger seemed to have a sixth sense for self-promotion. No sooner was he out of the cab than he held up a hand to pause the photographers, who had begun snapping away, so that he could find the vantage point from which his fabulousness would be best displayed. He found it at the top of the flight of steps leading to the Clubhouse, where he turned and leaned lazily against one of the recumbent bronze lions flanking the door, adjusting his pocket handkerchief and placing a hand artfully on his hip once again.

DALLY

It all seemed ridiculous to Charles, yet he had to admit Roger looked pretty good. In a kind of ridiculous way.

The locker room attendants had to be pressed into service to get Roger's luggage up to his room—or, rather, rooms, the one suite the clubhouse offered, normally reserved for visiting dignitaries. Roger looked around at his temporary home like he was smelling something bad, but kept his opinions to himself.

"Now, *Ro-zhay*," began Mrs. Carpenter, luxuriating in the French pronunciation of the boy's name, "if you're not too tired, we have a little luncheon planned for you in the dining room downstairs. Then, if you like, you and Charles could have a swim at the Downtown Athletic Club before we go on to meet Governor Smith later this afternoon. How does that sound?"

"*Ex*-Governor Smith," corrected Mr. Morgan, a Republican.

"Once a governor, always a governor," replied Mrs. Carpenter, thankful she didn't have to deal with Mr. Morgan except on state occasions like this one.

"That sounds vehry nice," said Roger.

Fifteen minutes later the group was assembled around a large round table in the dining room, where they feasted on chicken à la king over toasted English muffins followed by orange Jell-O salad with bananas and mandarin oranges submerged inside it. Roger spent the meal rearranging his food with his fork instead of actually putting any of it in his mouth. When the coffee service was winding down he picked up the bowl of brown and white sugar cubes and emptied it into the pocket of his suit coat. His hosts were too disconcerted by this gesture to ask its meaning.

"Do you think he's a *typical* French boy?" Mrs. Carpenter asked Mrs. Damrau in a conspiratorial whisper.

"I certainly hope not," replied Mrs. Damrau in a similarly hushed tone.

"Well, Roger, now it's on to the swimming pool, once you've had a chance to digest your meal," said Mr. Morgan.

"*Je suis desolé*," said Roger, "I just realized, in all my *bagage*s, I have not brought the attire for swimming. I did not know."

"Oh, that's all right," Charles said casually, oblivious to the invitation in his words. "We swim naked at the Downtown."

"*Nay-ked*," repeated Roger, searching his English vocabulary. Suddenly his face brightened.

"*Nu?*" he asked. "Then I am perfectly ready."

+   +   +

The Downtown Athletic Club had opened a few years earlier to great acclaim, and was already considered a masterpiece of the Art Deco style. Roger was suitably impressed with its stark white geometry and stylized decoration.

"*Très beau...très, très beau*," he said as the boys and Mr. Morgan moved from the immense lobby down the corridor to the Olympic-length pool, glittering in the sunlight that streamed in through a myriad of windows. Only a few lanes were occupied.

"The locker room is through those doors," the athletic director said with a nod of his head.

"Will you not join us, *Monsieur* Morgan?"

"No, no, not me. Too old, too fat. I'll be in the smoking lounge when you two have had your fill. Not too long, now. We have to get to Governor Smith's—ex-Governor Smith's, that is—by four."

Roger and Charles pushed through the swinging doors and found themselves the sole occupants of the pristine locker room. They undressed in silence and hung their clothes neatly in the large metal cubbies. Charles had done this hundreds of times before with other boys. Why did he suddenly feel self-conscious about getting undressed? Was it because Roger had taken his arm and then brushed the scratch on his face with his thumb? Maybe the French were just more touchy than Americans. He recalled hearing something about that in Social Studies class; the Romance peoples of Europe were more...what was the word? Demonstrative, that was it. Maybe that's what Roger was.

He closed his locker door to find Roger facing him, his arms folded across his chest. He wore two chains around his neck, one holding a cross, and the other some kind of religious medal. And nothing else. After Charles had just convinced himself that his uneasiness was merely the result of cultural differences he was hard-pressed to account for Roger's appraising stare that rolled up and down his naked body, making him feel doubly exposed.

"Let's go, no?" Roger said at the conclusion of his inspection.

"Let's go, yes," Charles said with a little sigh of resignation.

They each got a towel from the attendant seated behind a counter alongside the pool and made their way to the far end of the room, where they dropped them on the built-in bench and walked to the edge of the water.

"A race, yes?" said Roger.

And with that he plunged into the blue-green water, coming up into a perfect butterfly stroke that sent him flying down the lane. Charles was dumbstruck. He had never mastered the butterfly himself, but he was good at the crawl, the best in the Club, in fact, so he dived into the water fully expecting to close the gap between himself and the Frenchie in short order.

Charles swam his fastest, hardly taking a moment to look at where Roger might be until he got to the end of his lane and slapped the tile wall. Had he won?

No. There was Roger, halfway down the neighboring lane, on his return trip already.

"Fiddlesticks," said Charles.

After forty minutes of non-stop swimming Charles was exhausted. He climbed out of the water and sat on the edge of the pool, panting.

Roger swam up to him with a perplexed look on his face.

"You are all right?"

"Yeah, I'm just *tired*."

"So soon? But we have just started."

"Maybe you have, but I'm going to change."

Charles felt deceived as he made his way back to the locker room. The same boy who had placed his hand limply in Charles's was a first-class athlete. Why had he put on that show, then? What was the point?

Roger got out of the pool as well and ran to catch up with him. He took Charles's arm and draped it across his shoulders in a comradely manner. Once again, Charles was too surprised to protest. The pool had been chilly, and Roger's flank felt good and warm pressed up against his own.

"Thank you for the swim, Charles. It was very nice. I do not have a such big pool where I live."

"You're welcome," said Charles. "You're quite the swimmer."

"Yes, I am very good."

Charles laughed out loud at Roger's bluntness. He had been brought up never to praise himself, but Roger seemed simply to be stating a fact.

They showered in private stalls and then returned to their lockers to dry off. As Roger lifted one leg onto a bench to towel between his toes Charles found himself transfixed by the sight of his still-naked backside. To his horror, Roger turned his head at that moment and saw the direction of Charles's gaze, which he immediately redirected.

"Tell me about the medals you wear, Roger," said Charles, trying to sound casual even though his heart was racing.

"Of course."

He straightened and turned to face Charles, standing a little closer than Charles deemed necessary.

"This one is a cross, of course, and the other is *Saint Christophe*...how do you say? Saint Christopher. He is the *patron* of those who travel." He placed them in his palm and held them up for Charles to see. Charles could feel warm breath coming out of Roger's nostrils.

"Very interesting," he said, trying to sound business-like. "I'm a Presbyterian, so I'm afraid I don't know much about saints and all that..."

"Presby...what is that?"

"Uh, I don't know, really. I guess it's a kind of Protestant church."

Roger recoiled slightly at the sound of a word he recognized.

"*Protestant!*" he hissed, hastily scratching his chest in the sign of the Cross before adding, under his breath, "*Païens ...*"

"Um, how's that?"

Charles didn't know what to make of Roger's apparent distaste for his religion. He was relieved when the French boy shrugged and returned to his locker to dress.

+   +   +

At 3:15 they found Mr. Morgan in the smoking lounge and set out for the Empire State Building. After leaving politics Governor Smith had become the president of the corporation that built and managed the skyscraper, though he was still very much a presence behind the scenes, trying at every opportunity to thwart the policies of his fellow Democrat, Franklin Delano Roosevelt.

Mr. Morgan and the boys first visited the Observation Deck, where more photographers were waiting. Roger loved the panoramic views of the city, its rivers and harbor, and ran delightedly from side to side of the deck to take it all in. The photographers had a field day trying to keep up with him, and the reporters even asked for quotes.

"So Roger, what do you think of our city?"

"*C'est vraiment formidable*, fantastic! It's the dog's meow!"

"Can we quote you on that?"

"But of course."

At the stroke of four they were rejoined by Mrs. Carpenter and Mrs. Damrau and ushered through several outer offices into the *sanctum sanctorum* of Governor Smith's office, with its awe-inspiring plush carpets, gleaming wood cabinetry, and portraits of great men lining the walls of the room. Mr. Smith ground his cigar into the ashtray on his desk and rose to greet his guests. Mrs. Carpenter, who knew the governor socially, made the introductions.

"*Governor* Smith," she began, rather pointedly, "it's so very kind of you to take time in your busy schedule to receive us."

"Not at all, Gertie, not at all. Glad to do it."

Mrs. Carpenter winced at the sound of her Christian name. She much preferred Gertrude but couldn't seem to make it catch on.

"This is Mrs. Damrau, our matron, and Mr. Morgan, our athletic director, and Charles Whitehead, our president."

Each in turn approached the governor's desk and was given a hearty handshake.

"And *this*," she said, dramatically, "is Roger Charbonneau, our visitor from France."

Roger stepped up to the desk and pumped the governor's hand firmly and enthusiastically.

"Very pleased to meet you sir," he said in a noticeably huskier voice. "Very pleased indeed."

The governor nodded and smiled.

"What happened to the poofter?" Mr. Morgan whispered behind his hand to Mrs. Damrau.

"Beats me," she whispered back. "I guess he can turn it on and off."

"Sit down, sit down everyone, please."

The group looked about them and chose from the chairs scattered around the room. Mr. Smith pulled a chair up near his own and indicated that Roger should sit there.

"I've heard about you already, young man. You were on the maiden voyage of the *Normandie*. You set a speed record, you know. I like speed. Built this little pile in thirteen months, you know."

Roger dug in his pocket, pulled out a sugar cube, and popped it in his mouth.

"So, what'd you think of it? I'm interested in your opinion."

Roger thought for a moment, sucking on the sugar cube.

"I think *La Normandie* is the Empire State Building of sea ships."

"The..." The governor seemed astonished by this comparison. "Why, that's very good, very good indeed, my boy. I must find some way to use that. I understand you're off to see the President at the end of the week."

"Yes, sir."

"Well, it's always a great honor to meet a head of state but I'm sorry it has to be this particular incumbent. He's driving the country into the ground, you know."

Mrs. Carpenter squirmed in her chair, uneasy with the direction the conversation had taken. She was an ardent New Dealer herself. Mr. Morgan, however, felt his disdain for the ex-governor slipping away. Anybody who hated FDR couldn't be all bad.

"My boy, here are the principles I stand for:"

The governor raised one finger for each of them:

"Social mobility, economic opportunity, religious tolerance and individualism. The way I see it, it's a lot like your *liberté*, *égalité*, and *fraternité*. You've got to create the conditions that allow a man to rise to the top, no matter his origins, and then you've got to back off and let him sink or swim. This damned New Deal of Frank's is turning Americans into a bunch of lab rats waiting for their next free cookie. And you can tell him I said so!"

"I will!" said Roger, delighted to be given a mission. "Tell me again, if you please."

"Social mobility," said the governor holding up his fingers once again.

"Social mobility," repeated Roger, aping the governor's gestures.

"Economic opportunity."

"Economic opportunity."

"Religious tolerance."

"Religious tolerance."

"And individualism."

"Individualism. *Bon!* I have it!"

He took another sugar cube from his pocket and put it in his mouth.

Mr. Smith smiled gleefully at the thought of the stink bomb he would be setting off in his old rival's office come Friday. "Hey kid, you got one of those things for me?"

"But of course! *Brun ou blanc?* Brown or white?"

"I'll go with brown."

Roger took a brown cube from his stash and placed it on the governor's huge palm.

"*Voilà donc. Monsieur le gouverneur.*"

"Just call me Al."

+   +   +

On the ride back to the Clubhouse everyone heaped praises on Roger for his easy rapport with the governor. For the first time, he seemed genuinely humbled by their compliments.

"But you're *not* going to give the President that message, are you?" Mrs. Carpenter asked nervously. Before Roger could answer the cab had arrived at their destination.

It was now 5:30, and dinner would not be till 8:00, so Roger had some leisure for the first time since his arrival. He looked at Charles and nodded toward the elevator, indicating he should come up to the suite with him. Charles could see no good reason to do this, but he obediently followed Roger into the lift.

Over the next fifteen minutes the boys made only perfunctory conversation with one another, but Roger found every possible excuse to touch Charles lightly, turn him about, and manipulate him into the bedroom. If the doe-like expression on Charles's face was any indication, this was going to be almost too easy.

Once they were both in the bedroom, Roger opened his trunk and laid several ties on the bed.

"Which do you think *pour le dîner?*"

"Oh, gee, I'm not a very good judge of clothes. You dress much better than I do already."

"Let me see how they look on you," Roger said, snatching up the ties and coming around in front of Charles, who now stood with his back to the bed.

"This?" he asked, holding a tie to Charles's collar. "Or this?"

Charles, of course, could not see the ties and so could not venture an opinion, but he liked the feeling of Roger's fingers against his Adam's apple.

"Yes, this one. Zank you."

Roger laid his selection over the top of the trunk and turned back to Charles.

"You have been so kind to me all day, Charles. How can I thank you?"

Charles looked into Roger's face for a little too long before he shrugged and said: "I dunno. No need, I guess."

"But I would like to do *something* to express my appreciation."

He was practically cooing now.

Charles looked like he was about to explode at the unknown prospects opening out before him, so Roger decided the moment had come. He placed a hand on Charles's chest and pushed, gently but firmly. Charles fell backwards onto the bed as lightly as an autumn leaf to the ground. Before he could ask why Roger had done that he found himself being rapidly divested of his clothes. In one continuous, experienced gesture Roger unbuckled his belt, unfastened his pants, and yanked them along with his shorts down to his ankles.

"Wait," Charles protested, "what are you...oh...oh! OH!"

The last thing he remembered seeing was Roger's chestnut waves bobbing up and down between his legs.

Shortly thereafter an explosion went off in his brain and he blacked out.

When he came to, he was still lying on his back on Roger's bed and his pants were still down around his ankles, but some kind of robe and been draped over his torso. Roger was sitting in a chair by the window, reading.

"Wha...what happened?"

"You passed in..."

"Out?"

"Perhaps." Roger looked up from his book. "I hope eet was worth it."

Charles nodded groggily, not entirely sure what "eet" was. Throwing off the robe, which looked to be a dressing gown of Roger's, he sat up and hastily pulled up his underwear and pants, putting himself back together as quickly as he could given the comfortable lethargy of his limbs.

Roger put his book down and crossed to the bed. Crawling over it on all fours he kissed Charles gently on the lips. In spite of their encounter, Charles was dumbfounded by this gesture. Dumbfounded, but not displeased. Sensing this, Roger kissed him again. Finally grasping the value of this activity, Charles kissed Roger, which seemed to delight him.

"You are *très doux*, very sweet. Are all the American boys sweet like you?"

"Uh, yes. No! I'm not sure." Looking down at the crumpled bedspread he added: "No one ever called me sweet before."

"No?" Roger sat back on his heels, incredulous. "Not even *ta mère*, your mother?"

"Um, not that I can recall."

Roger leaned forward on his knuckles and grinned up into Charles's face. "Well, I must make up for all those silly people, must I not? You are sweet, Charles Whitehead! Sweet, sweet, sweet!"

With each repetition Roger kissed a different part of Charles's anatomy: his neck, his cheek, his ear. The last one made Charles giggle.

"Don't!" he said, flapping his hands to make Roger go away.

"I'm sorry, you don't like?"

"I meant, don't...stop," Charles said quietly, not sure if this was the right thing to say or not.

Roger looked at his watch. "Your mother will wonder where you are, I think."

A look of panic flashed across Charles's face.

"What time is it? How long have I been here? Oh, boy, I'm going to have a lot of trouble explaining this to Mom!"

He saw one of Roger's eyebrows shoot up.

"OK, maybe I'd better think of something else to tell her. But I should at least call her and tell him I'm all right. She worries."

"If you like," said Roger with a sly grin, "you can put me on the phone and I can tell her you are 'all right,' because you are *definitely* 'all right.'"

He ran his tongue sensuously across his upper lip, making Charles blush for the second time that day.

"Thanks, but no, I don't think you should do that. Where's the phone?"

Roger nodded his head in the direction of the living room. Charles made his way to it and lifted the receiver. The club operator came on the line.

"Darn it!" thought Charles. "There's a switchboard! She can hear everything I say if she wants."

"Number, please."

The voice sounded about a hundred years old, which was reassuring. She probably couldn't care less about Charles and his business.

"Fulham-6341, please."

"Please wait a moment while I connect you."

Roger walked through the living room.

"Tell her that you will come home to get some more clothes and then you will spend the night here at the Clubhouse."

"Spend the night…"

"Yes, spend the night. We will have so much fun."

The hand Charles was using to hold the receiver began to tremble.

"Oh, hi Mom! How are you? Sorry I'm not home yet. Something came up."

Roger guffawed and left the room.

"The Club wants me to stay here overnight so…so I can be ready to take Roger sightseeing tomorrow first thing. Yes, that's right. I'm coming home now to pack a bag and then I'll have dinner here with Roger and the committee."

Roger smiled to himself at his victory.

"What, Mom? Yes, he's very nice."

+   +   +

When "first thing" arrived the next morning Roger lay dozing peacefully in the bed wearing silk pajamas and a sleep mask over his eyes, while Charles sat huddled on the floor in a YMCA bathrobe, whimpering. He had had no idea his body could give him so much pleasure, so many times. Every time he thought about the events of the previous night he felt himself stiffen once more. Would he ever be able to get dressed again? For that matter, would he even be able to stand up? And those were just the practical considerations. What would his family and friends say about what he and Roger had spent the night doing? What would his *pastor* say? He was pretty sure this wasn't normal behavior for sixteen-year-old boys. Words he'd heard whispered in school hallways or shouted derisively in the boys' locker room floated unbidden to his consciousness: sissy, faggot, fairy, nancy boy, *one of them*. Was he now *one of them*? Was Roger?

As he wondered about this the boy in question raised a lazy hand to his face mask and lifted it a tiny crack.

"*Ah, tu voilà. 'Jour, chéri.*"

The sounds of Roger's voice snapped Charles out of his reverie.

145

"I have to look something up," he said, scrambling to his feet and darting into the suite's living room. So he could still stand up and walk, he realized. That was good.

Roger pulled the mask the rest of the way off his face and watched Charles's departure with curiosity. Were all American boys so business-like after *l'amour*?

Charles opened various drawers around the room, searching for the Bible he was sure the Y would have placed there. He found it in the top desk drawer and plopped down on the sofa, opening it on his lap, then realized he had no idea where to begin. Maybe there was an index at the back? But what word would he search out in the index? He knew he wouldn't find *sissy* or *faggot*. Yet he remained convinced that the answer he needed was somewhere in there.

Roger padded softly into the room and stood peering down at Charles, who did not look up from the book whose pages he was flipping through with increasing desperation.

"*Mais, qu'est-ce que tu fais?* What are you doing?"

Roger's question seemed to confirm the French boy's depravity. Charles lifted his head abruptly and stared disbelievingly into Roger's face. "It's the Bible, for heaven's sake! Don't you even know a Bible when you see one?"

Charles had intended this question to be dismissive, but Roger pondered an answer.

"Seen one..." He looked at the ceiling, searching his memory. "*Oui, probablement.* At Mass, in church, the big book on a stand at the front. But I don't think we're supposed to read it. That's what *les prêtres* are for."

"I'm pretty sure we are supposed to read it. What's a *prêtre*, anyway?"

Roger consulted his memory once more.

"Uh...priest. That's right. The priests read the Bible and tell us what it says."

Charles felt an unwelcome urge to have a priest suddenly materialize so he could tell them both what the Bible says about...this. He snapped the book shut with a bang and stood up, bringing himself eye to eye and disconcertingly close to Roger, who interpreted his proximity as an invitation and promptly cupped the back of Charles's head with one hand and pulled his mouth onto his own, thrusting his tongue into Charles's mouth in the most obscene way Charles could imagine.

So why was he just standing there? Because he'd never felt anything so good in his life.

When Roger finally finished mauling Charles's face he leaned his forehead against the American's, waiting for their breath to calm.

"That is a much better way to say good morning than...." He looked at the book lying closed on the sofa cushion. "Than trying to look things up in a book....even a holy one," he added, as a concession to Charles's sensibilities.

Charles let out a little sigh of defeat, vowing to find the answers he sought...later.

The boys showered and dressed and took the elevator to the cafeteria, which was already bustling with the early-morning workout types. Charles filled his tray with bacon and eggs, coffee and orange juice. Roger chose a single piece of toast and some tea. They sat down at a table beneath a sunny window.

Charles opened his mouth to say something about the day's itinerary when he realized that Roger had bowed his head and folded his hands on the table in front of him.

"*Notre Père, qui es aux cieux, que ton nom soit sanctifié.*"

Roger was praying! Charles couldn't understand the words but the rhythm of the prayer was unmistakable. He bowed his own head as he listened.

"*Que ton règne vienne, que ta volonté sot faite sur la terre comme au ciel.*"

Soon the entire room had become aware of the sound of a foreign language being recited with quiet piety, and conversation quickly ceased.

"*Donne-nous aujourd'hui notre pain de ce jour. Pardonne-nous nos offenses, comme nous pardonnons aussi à ceux qui nous ont offensés. Et ne nous soumets pas à la tentation, mais délivre-nous du mal. Amen.*"

Roger raised his head and emptied a packet of sugar into his tea, then another, before stirring it languidly. He looked around the room and was startled to see everyone looking back at him. He turned his head to the window to see if their interest had been piqued by something in the alley.

"Such beautiful faith," someone murmured, before everyone returned to their food and their conversations.

"You know the Lord's Prayer!" Charles exclaimed.

"Do I?" said Roger.

"Well, that's what we call it over here. It sounded very nice in French."

Roger gave Charles a wincing smile. "If you say so," he said.

+   +   +

For the next two days the boys were taken on a whirlwind tour of the city, from Radio City Music Hall to the Metropolitan Museum of Art, from Coney Island to Yankee Stadium, as well as to seemingly endless meetings with local French luminaries and politicians eager to hop on the Franco-American bandwagon. At each stop there were yet more interviews with Roger, who could be counted on to say something endearingly wrong each time, to the point that the papers started to publish anthologies of his goofs, one of them titled "French Onion Soup."

Their itinerary was exhausting enough, but in the intervals between each visit—and sometimes *during* the visit, if the men's bathroom door had a lock on it, or the local foliage afforded coverage—Roger had something new to teach Charles, who was proving an eager, if increasingly worn-out, pupil. He had decided he would do his biblical research when Roger was out of sight and less a source of temptation. Nevertheless, when Roger lured him into a clump of rhododendron bushes at the Central Park Zoo and tried to pull him to the ground, he finally rebelled.

"For gosh sakes, don't you ever *stop?*"

Roger looked up at him from the ground, a few blades of grass stuck in his hair. He tried his best to look and sound repentant. "OK, Charles, we stop. No more."

He propped himself on one elbow and slowly batted his eyes at Charles, who ignored the gesture for as long as he could, which turned out to be all of ten seconds.

"Oh! You're impossible!" he said, and threw himself on the ground next to Roger.

"Just go on with what you were doing, already."

+   +   +

Charles was learning numerous French phrases, none of which he could think of any possible use for in the future. What's more, he'd lost his stammer altogether, something he hadn't realized until Roger pointed it out.

"You don't have the *bégayement* so much anymore."

"The what?"

"I don't know the word in English. 'B...b...b....bienvenue.'"

"I don't?" Charles tried to remember the last time he had stammered. "By gosh, you're right!"

"I did that."

Charles laughed. "Yeah, and a few other things."

They were in Roger's suite at the Club the night of his farewell dinner, the implications of which they had not discussed. Charles's mother had rented him a tux for the occasion; Roger had brought his own, of course. When they had finished dressing they stood side by side in front of the mirror, deeply impressed with themselves.

"I have one more thing to teach you," Roger said, turning to his Dopp kit on the dresser.

"Roger, no! We just got dressed! We'll be late."

"It's not about that," he said, rifling through its contents. "I must teach you the correct way to wear *le parfum*."

"What's that? Perfume? I don't want any perfume."

"Don't worry, it's not for girls. *C'est eau de Cologne impériale*. It has been made the same way for many, many years, since the time of Bonaparte."

"I don't think I want to smell like Napoleon."

Roger held his right finger of the top of the cologne bottle and inverted it, then did the same with his left. He came chest to chest with Charles and reached up, putting the tiniest hints of fragrance behind each of his ears.

"Behind my ears? Wow. You sure know a lot of different things."

Roger suddenly became solemn.

"Yes. I know that I will not be happy to say goodbye to you, Charles Whitehead."

Charles shifted his weight from one foot to another, unsure of what to say. Suddenly, Roger burst into tears and threw his arms around him.

"*Tu me manques déja, chéri,*" he snuffled, stroking the back of Charles's head. Charles stood stiffly for a moment, remembering that Romance peoples tend to be demonstrative, but then he felt the moisture accumulating in the corners of his own eyes and wrapped his arms around Roger's slight frame.

"I don't know what you just said, but me, too, I think."

They hugged each other in silence for a long moment, then parted on a mutual signal.

"And there is something else I must say, an apology I must make."

"Apology?"

Charles felt genuinely surprised. During their short acquaintance Roger had maintained a supreme confidence in his every action. What could this be? "Yes."

Roger hesitated for a moment, collecting his thoughts. "My parents taught me that all those who are not Catholic are *païens*...I looked up the word in English: it's 'pagans.' But you do not seem like a pagan to me, and, if you are one, that does not seem like such a bad thing to be at all."

Charles wasn't sure how much of a compliment that was.

"But *le bon Dieu* is the God of love, is he not? So I know he loves you as...as I do, *Protestant* or no."

The tears had returned to Charles's eyes.

"Thank you," he said, wiping a hand across his wet cheeks. "I...I love you, too."

Roger inhaled stiffly through his nose, signaling the end of this exchange.

"OK, *on y va*," said Roger.

"*On y va*," agreed Charles, with such a good accent that Roger turned and stared.

+   +   +

The dining hall of the Clubhouse was festooned with flowers and greenery and packed with guests, some of whom had invited themselves. Roger had been a definite hit with New York City, and Charles's polite speech about leaving with many new American friends had proven prophetic. The boys were seated at the same table in recognition of Charles's yeoman's duty as a tour guide, but across from one another. Charles was seated next to Mrs. Carpenter.

"My, doesn't that centerpiece smell wonderful!" she exclaimed, leaning in to get a better whiff.

"Those are dahlias, Gertie," came a woman's voice from the other side of the table. "They don't have a scent."

"Well, then, what am I smelling?"

She looked at Charles and took a sniff in his direction.

"Charles Whitehead! Are you wearing perfume?"

"Uh, yes. No. Maybe."

"Boys' Club boys do not wear scent, young man!"

She looked balefully at Roger across the table.

"I'm beginning to think that French boy has been a bad influence on you."

If you only knew, Charles thought.

The menu had been prepared by a real French chef, and Roger would love to have eaten it with gusto, had he not been interrupted every time he raised his fork by yet another New Yorker who wanted to wish him well. He regretted not being friendlier earlier in his visit, because the Americans were certainly *all right*. As that thought crossed his mind he looked across the table at Charles and thought he might start to cry again. Some Americans were even more all right than others, and that was a fact. Another greeter at his elbow helped him banish the tears.

After dinner there were the usual speeches about international friendship and gratitude to all who had made the visit such a success, and so on, and so on, and then it was time for Roger to speak.

"*Mes amis*, my friends, it has been my great joy to spend these three days in your *formidable* city of New York. So many things to see and do, I think one could live to be a very old man and not see and do them all!"

A murmur of self-satisfaction ran through the listeners.

"Indeed, if one were not able to live in Paris, one could do no worse than to live in New York!"

This did not sound very flattering and Roger looked up from his notes in time to see that on the faces of the audience.

"No *better*, was my meaning. I am often confused by those two words."

Relieved laughter rippled through the room.

"As I travel to your nation's capital to meet your great *président* I take with me many happy memories of my time in your wonderful city. Such memories are worthless to me."

Roger's speech was proving to be something of a roller coaster ride. A French national came up to the podium and whispered in Roger's ear. He whispered into hers and she whispered back and then returned to her table.

"*Je vous en prie.* Such memories are *priceless* to me!"

Someone let out a howl from the back of the room, and there was a smattering of applause.

"I thank all of you for your kindness to me, and wish you all my very best. But I would be remiss if I did not say a special word of thanks to Charles Whitehead, who in just three days has become my good friend, *mon copain*. Thank you for everything *mon ami*, and I do mean everything."

Charles blushed and smiled as the room applauded him, blissfully unaware of what they were acknowledging.

"So, *ça y est,* thank you again, good night and good bye! *Bonsoir et adieu!*"

With a little wave Roger left the podium and returned to his seat as the audience stood for a final ovation. A waitress who thought Roger was pretty cute had left him a second *île flottante* since he hadn't been able to eat the first one with so many interruptions. He tucked into it with gusto.

As the guests started to take their leave Osgood Renssalaer, the national president of the Boys' Clubs of America, made his way across the room to where Charles was sitting. Charles got up from his chair and waited expectantly to hear what Mr. Renssalaer might say. The older man clapped Charles on the shoulder and said in his most avuncular voice:

"Charles, you've been such a great companion to Roger this week, we've decided to pay your way to accompany him to Washington to meet the president. There's no point in making him start all over again with a new crowd. Whaddya say?"

Charles puffed out his cheeks and made a long, whistling exhalation, wondering whether he'd still be alive by Friday, or just a little pile of dust and ashes. He was happy either way.

The Ballad of Charlie and James

April, 1937
Bogdon Holler, West Virginia

No one was quite sure when the boys had arrived in Bogdon Holler, or where they'd come from. One day the old Darby cabin was in an advanced state of dilapidation, and the next two young men could be seen making repairs and getting the place habitable once more. Everyone was curious about the strangers but no one asked by what right the boys had taken possession of Darby's place. The old man had died without kin; was one of them some distant relative? How else would they know about the cabin? Everyone figured they'd need supplies sooner or later, and then the mystery would be solved.

And sure enough, that's how it came about. One morning in mid-April the two boys came striding into town looking for all the world like two young Charles Lindberghs, wearing identical leather bomber jackets, white shirts open at the collar, and corduroy britches tucked into knee-high lace-up boots. One was taller and seemed older than the other. He had sandy hair combed back from his forehead, a thin moustache, and perfect features like a model in a catalogue. The other boy, younger and shorter, was a ginger, his hair a mass of auburn curls on top of his head, the sides cropped short, and freckles all over his face, which was that of a pugilist. Both of them looked pretty humorless, but the younger one seemed like he would cut you dead if you looked at him wrong. They walked quickly and purposefully down the town's only street as though they knew the place, and clambered up the three wooden steps into Chauncey Graves's general store without slowing their pace. A small crowd followed them through the door, gawking. The expression of the older boy softened as soon as he engaged the owner.

"Good morning," he said, flashing a sudden smile, announcing himself an outsider in three syllables.

"A *jasper!*" rippled through the assembled folk in hushed and surprised tones.

"Morning to ye," said Chauncey. "What can I do ye fer?"

"Well, as a matter of fact, we have a list."

As a matter of fact now got passed from mouth to ear among the onlookers.

"A *fancy jasper!*" one of them said. The phrase seemed to arouse the ire of the ginger, who turned on the crowd behind him.

"Yeah, he's a jasper, but he ain't no fancy jasper!"

Hearing the cadences of the holler delighted and perplexed the listeners. "What's this young'un doing with a jasper?" they said to one another. Most foreigners who showed up here were either lost or taking photographs of the locals' 'misery' on a WPA grant. They sure didn't come to live here.

"Hit were none of yore lookout what we's fixin' to buy for ourselves in no case. Don't you'uns need to be a-workin'? Go on, scat now!"

"About that list," the first young man said, sounding more urbane than ever after his companion's outburst.

"Fraid readin's not strong with me," Chauncey said. "If you might could speak it out, we'll jes' see how I can help ye."

"Of course," said the young man, and began to read the long inventory aloud, sending the proprietor from one end of the store to the other gathering everything from flour to nails to fabric for curtains.

The fierce glare that accompanied the ginger's injunction to "Scat!" had by now largely emptied the store, and he turned back to his companion to whisper something in his ear. "Don' forget now, Charlie..." was all Chauncey could make out of this communication as he measured out nine yards of bleached muslin.

"Thank you, James," said Charlie with a slight smile, as though they were sharing a private joke. "I hadn't forgotten."

James pivoted on his heel so his back was to the counter. He laid his elbows on top of it and struck a lounging pose.

"You done forgot last time, cuz I weren't there to remind ye."

"You're right," said Charlie good-naturedly. "I did."

He raised his voice to the storekeeper.

"And a pound of those good-looking horehound drops from that jar over there, if you please."

"A pound!" Chauncey exclaimed. "You boys must have quite the sweet toofs."

"Well, one of us does," Charlie said quietly as a tiny smile flickered across the other young man's face.

By the time all the items had been read out a considerable pile had risen next to the cash register. Chauncey began to wonder if they were good for the bill, but figured he would take one of those leather jackets in trade for cash on the barrel.

"Sorry I h'aint got nary none o' that twine today. I'll get me s'more on Friday."

"Friday. Very good," said Charlie. "What do we owe you?"

"Fixin' to run a tab, was you?"

The question was exploratory.

"That won't be necessary."

The young man pulled a bulging wallet from inside his jacket. Chauncey had never seen crocodile skin before.

"Whoo-ee!" he whistled softly. "What in tarnation critter gave up its life to make you that there thing?"

Charlie seemed surprised by the question. He followed Chauncey's gaze to the wallet.

"This? Oh, it's crocodile skin."

Chauncey looked blank.

"Don't think we have none of them in these parts."

"No, probably not. Perhaps alligators? *'Gators?'*"

Charlie prided himself on having the common touch.

"Nope, none of those, neither. That'll be eighteen dollars even, if ye please."

Charlie removed two tens and handed them to Chauncey.

"Please just keep the change."

"Keep it?"

Chauncey looked perplexed.

"Nobody never offered to pie me more then I asked afore."

Charlie didn't want to seem condescending.

"Shall we just say it's to cover the twine on Friday?"

"Still have a good bit left over," said Chauncey, sounding doubtful.

"Well, then, toward our future purchases. Thank you, Mr...?"

"Chauncey."

"Mr. Chauncey."

"Nope, just Chauncey."

"Very good."

The storekeeper made two bundles of the supplies and the young men headed out the door.

"Ought not to have done that," James said as they headed back down the road to the cabin.

"Done what?"

"Tol' him to keep the change. Folks 'round here is tetchy."

"Touchy? About what?"

"The dole," James said. "It always the beginnin' o'the end."

They carried on in silence for a ways after that. The cabin was about two miles outside of town—more, or less, depending on what you considered the town limits—hidden in a clearing carved out of a dense forest of pine, hickory and oak. Darby's will laid claim to five surrounding acres, but it was unlikely the county had any document on file to attest to that. In any case, less than half an acre had been cleared, and that seemed to suffice the boys.

The cabin consisted of a large main room, dominated by a stone hearth, that served as living room, dining room and kitchen, and a bedroom that had been an add-on to one side of the structure. Darby had dug a good well a few feet from the front door, and once the pump had been cleaned and oiled the groundwater flowed clear and plentiful again. In spite of years of neglect Darby's few pieces of furniture were still serviceable, and after the boys had repaired and spruced it all up they built some bookshelves from the pile of discarded wood they'd found out back, most of it rotting but enough useable to suit their purposes. Charlie lined up his law books on them, giving the place a downright clubby look.

"Never had no books around me afore," James had commented. His mother had taught him to read, but otherwise most of his formal education had been piecemeal and ineffective. He found the presence of the books intimidating.

"Would you like me to help with your reading?" Charlie had volunteered. "We won't use these, of course," he said, sweeping a hand over the law books. "Too boring. Maybe we can find a good novel somewhere, or even some comic books."

"Comic books? What're those?"

"Books with pictures in them, lots of pictures of what the words are saying."

James nodded solemnly, intrigued by this idea.

After they'd stowed away all the new supplies it was time to think about dinner. They each took rifles and slung them over their shoulders before leaving the cabin to check the traps they laid each day. James had taught Charlie how to lay them in a circular pattern around the cabin so they could be checked systematically without any getting overlooked. The guns were for anything else viable they might see in the course of their rounds.

They met an hour later and pooled their prizes: Charlie had found a quail in one trap and a possum in another; James had shot a cottontail. Meat for the next three days, at least. Charlie was still squeamish about cleaning their victims, but once James had taken care of this unpleasant task he took over and made a stew of all three, augmenting it with carrots and potatoes. They ate at the small dining table, surrounded by lantern and firelight.

It was James's turn to do the dishes. Charlie threw a log on the fire and sat down to continue his reading of the second volume of *Tort Law of West Virginia*. He was an unusually fast reader, able to scan the page with one eye while he kept the other on James. When he saw that he'd come to the final dish to dry, Charlie closed the book, stood up and crossed the room. He wrapped his arms around James's waist from behind and squeezed him tightly, planting a kiss on his left ear at the same time. James continued to wipe the dish in spite of the fact that it was already dry. Charlie changed the kiss to a nip.

"Ow," James protested.

"James!" Charlie said, feigning wounded feelings. "Is that any way to respond to your Charlie? Huh? The one who took you in when no one else would? Who buys your clothes and tools, that bow and arrow set you wanted, and anything else your heart desires?"

James finally placed the dish in the rack with the others.

"I got us this here cabin."

"You did, you did do that. And I'm very grateful. In fact, I'd like to show you how grateful I am."

James knew what that meant, and shuddered. Ignoring the sudden stiffening of the younger man's body, Charlie raised his hands from James's waist to his throat and began unbuttoning his shirt. When he'd gotten halfway down he reached inside and pinched James's nipple lightly before circling it teasingly with one finger. Receiving no response, he resumed unbuttoning the shirt, pressing his groin into James's backside a little harder with each button.

When he'd gotten the shirt open Charlie yanked the shirt tails out of James's pants and pulled down on the collar, exposing the younger man's freckled back. He removed first one arm and then the other from its sleeve, then ran an approving hand over James's broad shoulders.

"Beautiful," he murmured.

He kissed one of James's shoulder blades.

"Perfect."

James caught a glimpse of the two of them in the black glass of the small window over the sink and quickly looked away again. He thought about how much wood he ought to chop tomorrow, and what he might find caught in the traps. Maybe they'd finally score a coon; he missed the taste of coon meat.

Charlie yanked James's belt strap one way and then the other, opening the buckle, and pulled it through the loops with a snap.

"I'll bet we *might could* find a use for this later," Charlie said.

"No!" James replied, angry. "I ain't done nothin' wrong."

"Nothing except be so god-damned fetching," Charlie purred. "Sometimes beauty like yours needs a little punishment to keep it from getting conceited."

"I never knows what the hell yore talkin' about," James muttered.

Still pressing hard against his backside, Charlie began to open the buttons of James's britches one by one, top to bottom, his breath becoming heavier with each release. He pulled James's pants down and let them fall around his feet, still tucked into his boots. He caressed each of James's buttocks in turn before spanking them lightly, then tugged at his red boxer shorts and brought them slowly down to join the pile of corduroy at James's feet. Dropping to his knees, he spread the other's buttocks apart and thrust his face between them, inhaling deeply. James braced himself by extending his arms along the cold edge of the metal sink, hoping this part would not last long tonight.

Charlie eventually pulled his head out and stood, pushing James out of the way of the sink. James stumbled and nearly fell with his pants twisted around his ankles.

"Take those things off and go wait for me in the bedroom," Charlie said, no longer purring. He poured some water into the sink from the bucket and washed his lips off with the Fels-Naptha soap bar James had used to wash their dishes. Then he joined James in the bedroom.

James had lit the candle on the bedside table, just as he'd been taught. Charlie sat to take off his boots, then removed his clothes and threw them over a chair. He came and stood at the foot of the bed, looking at James lying naked on top of the sheets, his legs bent at the knee.

"Come, James, let us worship the Lord together."

Charlie climbed on the bed and knelt between James's legs, slowly spreading them apart. Then he placed a hand on the back of each of his thighs and pushed until his legs were practically over his head. James neither resisted nor participated in Charlie's manipulation of his body. His eyes followed Charlie's face dispassionately, as though he were trying to discern his thoughts but did not much care whether he was successful in the endeavor.

Keeping James's legs aloft by placing an elbow across them, Charlie reached into the drawer in the bedside table and grabbed the bottle of Johnson's baby cream. Pushing a bit harder on James's legs, Charlie worked a scoop of it into James's crack and then slathered his stiff penis. James winced as the cool lotion hit his warm flesh.

"No kissin'," he said, softly but defiantly.

"No kissing," Charlie repeated before stretching himself between James's legs and covering the younger man's mouth with his own, working a finger insistently into James's insides at the same time. In spite of his warning, James's mouth responded to the pressure of Charlie's, however unwillingly. Charlie didn't care. He pushed himself inside of James and began to thrust, harder and harder, lost in a red haze of lust as the tightness of James's passage worked its reliable magic on his member. He seemed oblivious of James's pain, a pain so great it made him grip the sides of the bed till his knuckles turned white and tears ran down his cheeks, pain of the body and of the soul, pain so ancient he could no longer remember a time when it did not rule his nights.

When Charlie had finally spent himself he jerked roughly out of James's body and brought the silent young man to a joyless climax before fetching a towel to clean them both off. When he turned back to the bed James was looking down the length of his body at him.

"Hif you ever lie a hand on me agin, I swear I'll keel you."

Charlie made no response to this threat as he cleaned the sticky semen from James's belly. When he finished he tossed the towel in the corner of the room and climbed into bed.

"Praise the Lord for all his mercies," he said, and blew out the candle.

+ + +

Charlie and James had walked into town as though they'd known the place because, in fact, one of them did. Old Man Darby had been James's mother's third cousin thrice removed, and when James was a child they had come to visit. It had not been a social call. James's mother had reached her limit with her husband's drinking and belligerence. The first years of their marriage had been happy enough, but when James came along with his dark red hair, his father grew suddenly cold, knowing no such coloring had ever shown up in his family or his wife's. He accused her of unfaithfulness and began to beat her and, as soon as he was able to run about, the child as well. He left the other children alone, reserving his rage for his wife and her supposed bastard. As the years passed it got to be more than she could stand. So she took ten-year-old James and went to Bogdon Holler on the advice of another cousin, hoping a relative she'd never met could provide her boy with sanctuary. It was not to be. Everlast Darby was a confirmed bachelor approaching the end of his life, cantankerous and set in his ways. He'd let them stay a few days, but had no desire to assume responsibility for his young cousin, even to save his life. Yet that short visit proved a revelation to James, the longest stretch of time he could recall when his father wasn't yelling or hitting or threatening him or his mother. He explored the town, charming everyone he met with his red curls and sweet demeanor. He had his first horehound drop at Chauncey Graves's general store, and it made his eyes grow bright. He wanted to stay forever; he cried when his mother told him they had to leave. But the trip had not been in vain. Fully aware of the corruption growing in his lungs, Everlast wrote out a will leaving the cabin and its land to James, and gave a copy to his mother to keep. Four years later, when her own lungs began to fail, she'd given it to James, then left this world without a murmur, finally succumbing to her exhaustion.

His mother's death marked a turning point in James's relationship to his father, already troubled enough. Lacking a wife, his father took his abuse of James in a new direction, satisfying his lust on the handsome young teenager he considered an interloper in his home. The life nearly crushed out of him after two years of cruelties—inflicted by way of a leather belt, spittle, and plenty of hooch—James found a last dying ember of hope, took the will from beneath a floorboard, and fled the only home he'd ever known.

+   +   +

"Whar's the meetin' house, then?" James asked the young man he'd struck up an idle conversation with outside of the general store on Friday afternoon when he'd gone to fetch the newly-arrived twine.

"It be thar," said the boy, thrusting his chin toward a rickety bell tower with a cross listing precariously on its modest summit. "Why d'ye ask?"

"I'm aimin' to preach there, if'n the parson'll have me."

The boy whistled. "You a preacher, then, are ye? Never saw no preacher my own age afore this."

James looked reflectively at the sky. "That's cuz ye h'aint seen me afore this." He dragged his toe in the dust of the road, writing mysterious figures like Jesus with the adulterous woman's accusers. "Know where I might find the parson, this time of day?"

"Prob'ly out back of the Climson barn, drinkin' hooch."

James considered the patterns he'd drawn in the road. "Show me," he said.

The parson, red-faced and bleary-eyed, was glad enough to have a guest preacher, even an unknown and probably unqualified one. Might make him look good.

"You got you the gift, boy? You sure o'that?"

"The Holy Ghost were given me in nineteen and thirty-three an' I been preachin' ever since."

"Well, a-righty, then. See you at meetin', five o'clock this Sunday."

"Five?" James asked, raising his eyebrows. "H'aint that kind o'late for church?"

"Gives me more time to recover," said the reverend, raising a fist to his closed mouth to suppress a belch.

+   +   +

If the town had been intrigued before by the solemn-looking ginger who'd come into town with the foreigner, they were agog to hear him preach, news of which had been spread by the boy who'd taken James to make his inquiry. Teenage evangelists were in no short supply in this part of West Virginia, but they always seemed to pass Bogdon Holler right by, apparently convinced the town was beyond saving. Or maybe they just couldn't find it on a map.

Attendance was double that Sunday evening as more of the menfolk showed up to join their wives and children at worship instead of gathering in groups somewhere down the street to smoke or chew till the service was over. The reverend looked redder in the face than usual, and everybody in the congregation knew that thing going around his mouth was not chaw (he wouldn't dare) but a piece of boiled pine bark to freshen his breath and mask the odor of hooch, something it failed to accomplish. A little after five the parson stood and began the service.

"Praise Jesus!" he called out.

"Praise Jesus," the congregation answered dutifully.

"No, I said 'Praise *Jesus!*'" he repeated, reproachfully.

"Praise JESUS!" the congregation offered, a bit more enthusiastically.

"I said 'PRAISE JESUS'!" shouted the parson, finally sounding like he believed it himself.

"PRAISE JESUS!" the congregation shouted back, warming to the game.

"Well, amen to that. Praise Jesus that we have with us this evenin' a fine young preacher by the name of...of..."

He'd failed to ask James his name. He looked inquiringly toward the young man seated across from him on the dais up front of the church.

"James Monroe, sir," he supplied.

"James Monroe?" the parson said, sounding disconcerted. "Like the president?"

"Yes, sir."

"Any relation?"

"No, sir."

The parson regained his momentum.

"Well, praise Jesus that we have young James Monroe, no relation, to preach the Word of God to us tonight. Please mind him, now."

He took his seat again, hoping this kid wasn't going to get him fired.

The congregation settled into the hard pews, grateful for any novelty that might come their way. Looking solemn and concentrated, James rose from his chair and crossed to the center of the dais, clasping a worn Bible in his hands. He took a long moment to scan every face in front of him, nodding thoughtfully, before he opened his mouth.

"Truth will stand when the world is on far," he said quietly.

The congregation leaned in, not certain of what they'd heard.

"Truth will stand when the world is on *far*," he repeated, louder this time.

"Amen to that," someone called out.

"And what is that truth that will stand when the world is on far?" he asked, rhetorically. "I will tell you, my friends. It is this."

He opened his Bible with a violent snap and glanced down at the text.

"'The unrighteous shall not inherit the kingdom of God.' That's what Saint Paul says in First Corinthians, Chapter six, verse nine. 'Know ye not that the unrighteous shall not inherit the kingdom of God?' But what does he mean by sayin' this? Who are the 'unrighteous'? Anyone amongst us here tonight?"

An unaccustomed shiver of pleasure went through the congregation. The parson could whoop with the best of them, but he never made them feel like miserable sinners, and they longed to be convicted.

"Anyone? Well, listen to this, then. 'Be not deceived,' says the apostle, 'neither fornicators, nor idolaters, nor adulterers, nor effeminate, nor abusers of themselves with mankind, nor thieves, nor covetous, nor drunkards, nor revilers, nor extortioners, shall inherit the kingdom of God!'"

James's voice had risen with each category on the list. He ran his tongue around his lips, gathering momentum.

"Any of this soundin'—*familiah*—to any of you'uns?" he asked, the merest hint of a smile on his face. "Any you men sleepin' with someone he ain't married to? How's about you gals? Well?"

The congregation beamed at his daring, confident that as a visitor he couldn't possibly know the answer to his questions.

"What about drunkards? We got any drunkards here with us tonight?"

The men in the congregation laughed uneasily while everyone tried to avoid looking at the parson.

"No, sir!" someone called. "We's all sober as judges!"

A general guffaw went up from the crowd.

"How about coveters? Ladies, when you look at the Sears Roebuck, you see anything you want?"

A titter ran through the women.

"Or, maybe I should put it this-away: You see anything you *don't* want?"

The room erupted in laughter and applause.

"*No*," called one long-suffering husband seated in the back.

"What about pansy boys? You got any of them?"

"No, sir!"

"Any idolaters?"

"No, sir!"

"Any of you men 'abusing yourselves' one t'other?"

"NO, SIR!" the men shouted back, not quite sure what they were denying.

"Well, then, how about thieves? There's gotta be some sticky fingers out there!"

"NO!" they cried, thoroughly enjoying themselves.

James rocked back on his heels, one hand in his pants pocket.

"Well, then, I guess everybody here is ready to inherit the kingdom of God!"

"Praise Jesus!" "Thy kingdom come, Lord!"

An extended celebration ensued, punctuated by ejaculations and clapping and even a few ecstatic tongues. James grinned at them for a long moment, waiting till the gaiety subsided. Eventually the noise died down and the congregation looked toward James once more, giddy with expectation. He surveyed all their faces a final time, then spoke:

"Well, ye ain't gonna," he said, in a murderous but perfectly audible whisper.

The room became deadly quiet.

"An' ye know why? Cuz ye are all a bunch of God...damned...lars."

The congregation sat in stunned silence, unsure of whether he meant what he'd just said or had plans to pull the rug out from under them once again.

"Truth will stand when the world is on far," James concluded. He walked down the aisle and out the front door of the church. When he'd gotten about a block away he heard the congregation erupt in applause, and paused a moment to bask in his accomplishment. Yes, sir, he had the gift all right.

+   +   +

Charlie had offered to come hear James preach but felt relieved when James discouraged him. As an Episcopalian and an Ohioan, he figured he'd probably be out of his depth, anyway. Instead, he studied his law books and contemplated how he'd come to be studying them in a mountain holler in West Virginia, probably the last place he'd have chosen for himself.

He'd been a third year law student at Capital University in Columbus when the dean walked in on him humping the newest whiz kid assistant professor one night and promptly sent them both packing. (What, exactly, the dean had been doing entering the professor's home at night was a question that remained unaddressed.) The school had phoned his wealthy parents in Shaker Heights before he could and explained the circumstances of his dismissal, apparently in lurid detail, with the result that they'd sent him a hefty check and told him not to bother coming home. So he'd settled on West Virginia, figuring it couldn't be that hard to pass the bar in a state where so many were illiterate.

He'd planned to make his way to Charleston, but at the train station in Huntington he'd spied James sitting on a bench looking lost. He sat down a foot away from him and waited for the younger man to notice him, but James continued to stare straight ahead, apparently lost in thought. Charlie took a bag of peppermints out of his satchel and held it out toward James, who finally turned in his direction, his eyes on the bag.

"Peppermint?"

James looked uncertain, but he hadn't eaten in days. "I don't care."

Charlie didn't realize the phrase meant "yes" in this part of the world and started to withdraw the bag when James grabbed at it and took three peppermints, stuffing them hungrily into his mouth.

"Whoa, there! They're not food, you know. Just take one at a time, and suck on it."

His advice came too late. Charlie realized the boy was hungry. "Where are you headed?"

James mumbled something, his mouth full of the mints.

"Sorry, I didn't quite catch that."

"Dunno," James finally said, swallowing the remnants of the mints. "Got no money for a ticket."

"No money..." Charlie repeated. "Then why are you here at the station?"

James shrugged. "Thought somebody might hep me."

Charlie took stock of James's compact body, sweet freckled face, and wild red curls.

"I think someone just might," he said. "Let's find ourselves something to eat."

Had no one ever warned James about strangers? Apparently not. Charlie had no way of knowing that there were no strangers in this young man's life, only family members, and they were so dangerous that it would be hard to imagine a stranger doing worse. So James had accompanied Charlie out of the station to a restaurant, and poured out his life story over copious amounts of fried chicken and biscuits and giblet gravy to this young man his elder by three or four years whom he'd known for less than an hour.

That night Charlie got them a hotel room, careful to ask for twin beds so as not to arouse the clerk's suspicion. Before the night was over he had joined James in his, taking him in his arms and caressing his hair. He could tell that James liked that, but he went no further.

Their stay in Huntington extended day after day. James admired Charlie's clothes, so Charlie bought him his own to match. He confided his love of horehound drops, and Charlie bought those, too, and virtually everything else James laid an admiring eye upon. James could hardly believe his luck. He soon realized he'd need some place to put all the possessions he was acquiring besides the shopping bags they'd come in, so he confided in Charlie about the cabin in Bogdon Holler. And that was how he'd come to be reading law smack in the middle of hillbilly nowhere. (The other details of their shared life—like the fact that James's trembling recital of his father's abuse had aroused Charlie's lust instead of his pity, or the mounting evidence that James had no natural inclination toward Charlie and certainly no enjoyment in his nightly humiliations—had not given Charlie a moment's pause in the execution of his every desire. The future lawyer slept with a clear conscience.)

James returned from church around six-thirty. He entered the room with a spring in his step, full of himself.

"What's for dinner?" he asked eagerly, knowing full well it would be stew again.

"Well, someone's had a good evening! The preaching went well, I take it?"

"I'd say so. People clapped. A long time, too."

"Excellent! Did you save souls tonight?"

Charlie had a mischievous glint in his eye, but James considered the question for a moment. "I think so," he said thoughtfully. "Yes, I'd say I did."

"Good, good. Let's eat. Everything's hot."

As the meal progressed, James's ebullience began to wane. In church he'd been somebody, a *preacher*, someone people listened to and thought about his words. Here, in the cabin, his words meant nothing, especially words like "no" and "stop." When Charlie placed a baked apple in front of him his heart began to race and his breath became shallow, because he knew that when the last dish was cleaned up any damn shameful thing might follow. He wanted Charlie out of his house, out of his life, but couldn't see any way to make it happen. If he went to the sheriff, he'd want to know what was wrong, and then he'd have to tell him what all they'd been doing, and he could never, ever do that.

By nine Charlie had James naked and bent over a chair, his hands and feet bound to its legs by the twine he'd gone in to town to pick up that afternoon. Charlie spent a long time just looking at him this way, seated on another chair and stroking the cock he'd pulled out of his pants. Then he stood up, took James's belt, and started to bring it down with all his strength on his exposed backside.

"Charlie, stop!" James pleaded. "I ain't done nothin' wrong!"

The belt came down again, harder. Welts were rising on James's buttocks.

"You let your father do this to you, didn't you? And he *beat* you and *hit* you and *swore* at you." Down came the belt again.

"I didn't *let* him, he just *did* it!" James had begun to cry, his tears pooling on the chair seat beneath him.

"Well, if you let your father do this and he was a bastard, how much more should you offer me the same opportunities, who treats you nicely and buys you everything you want." Some of the welts had begun to ooze blood. "Besides, you know you like it."

"*Like* it? I *hate* it! I HATE IT!" Mucus had begun to fall in great gobs from James's nose, pooling with his tears.

Charlie considered taking James in this position but found the angle of his backside too awkward, so he took his penknife and cut the twine. "Get into the bedroom."

James straightened himself with difficulty. The searing pain in his buttocks made it difficult to walk. He stumbled into the bedroom and closed the door.

Charlie started blowing out the lights but then remembered a reference in the third volume of Tort Law he needed to check; he looked it up, repeated it twice to commit it to memory, then turned out the last light and entered the darkened bedroom.

Seconds later, a rifle shot shattered the peaceful spring night. Another shot followed, and the sound of the rifle falling to the ground. A startled nighthawk abandoned its pursuit of a moth and flapped its wings wildly, anxious to be anywhere else it could find.

Boola, Boola!

25 September 1969

> *Any Yale man who f—s a Yale woman is too lazy to masturbate.*

The words were scrawled on the wall above the urinal Marty was using in a men's room at Sterling Library. It had only recently become a men's room, because until last month (with a few discreet exceptions) all the bathrooms at Yale had been men's rooms. Now they had designations, because women had been admitted as students—for the first time ever.

The meanness of the message bothered Marty. Besides, the women had only just arrived; who would have had the opportunity to evaluate their collective...desirability? Marty suspected that the author's sentiment was defensive and not based on experience. But what, exactly, was he defending himself from? Everyone Marty knew thought going co-ed was a great idea—overdue, in fact. Were they all lying? Saving their truest thoughts for the men's room wall? Or was this creep a solo act?

Marty zipped up his pants and headed for the sinks. Two guys he didn't know pushed the swinging door open and took their places at the urinals.

"Hey, look at this!"

One of the guys nodded in the direction of the graffiti. The other guy read it and laughed.

"So true, so true!"

Then they both laughed.

Yale men, Marty thought as he left the bathroom. A proud tradition.

He emerged from the Gothic gloom of the library into the radiance of a perfect late September afternoon, warm in the sun, chilly in the shade, the trees just starting to show a few glimmers of color. He stopped and turned his face to the sky, his eyes closed, basking in the rays and trying to commit everything to memory—the lively murmur of conversation from students seated on the grass, the distant whoosh of car traffic, the occasional bird song. This would be his last autumn in New Haven, and he wanted to remember it always.

Leighton would probably roll his eyes and tell him he was being soft.

Leighton Albright was Marty's best friend at Yale and one of his suite mates at Branford College. They'd had almost no classes together, since Leighton was an American History major and Marty was Political Science, but they were both on the cheerleading squad and sang in the Battell Chapel choir,

Marty a baritone and Leighton a tenor. When they'd met freshman year, Leighton had been unable to repress a sniff upon learning that Marty was a scholarship student. He himself was third generation legacy, and believed strongly that Branford should be limited to his peers, but President Brewster had done away with that system, so Leighton just had to suck it up and shake hands with poor people. In spite of their rocky start, they discovered a mutual obsession with the Yankees while they waited for their cheerleader auditions, and soon enough they'd forgiven each other's sins.

When Marty had drunk his fill of Ivy ambience he hopped a bus for the Bowl, where the cheerleading squad would have its last intense rehearsal before the Yale-Dartmouth game coming up in two days. Alums, parents, and hangers-on from all over would descend on the town. Yale had won the last three match-ups, but a number of key players had graduated off the team in the spring and a lot of the new ones seemed injury-prone, so the outcome this year was anybody's guess. Coach Robins had called a special meeting of the cheer squad before practice began to discuss the impending arrival of women on the team. The team wouldn't actually have any say in the matter, of course—everyone knew which way the wind was blowing with Brewster at the helm—but Robins wanted to give the boys a chance to let off some steam.

As it turned out, some of them saw distinct advantages:

"How soon can we get some chicks on the squad?" asked Charlie. "I'm tired of catching Brodie all the time...he eats too many potatoes at dinner."

"Shut up, Charlie!"

"Gentlemen!" Coach Robins said.

"He doesn't have boobs, either," Mason chimed in.

"Gentlemen, please! Watch your language."

"Sorry, Coach. Brodie has no *breasts*."

"He will if he keeps up with the potatoes."

"Lay off already."

"I don't know," said Cooper. "It feels really odd to think about doing some of the moves we do with girls. It would start to seem, you know..." Cooper lowered his voice. "...*sexual*."

"Ooooo!" hooted the squad in unison.

"Cooper said a dirty word."

"Isn't that the point?" asked Leighton. "What's wrong with sexual?"

"Well, nothing, the way you say it. But the way Cooper says it...I'm in."

The coach cleared his throat.

"Boys, I didn't call this meeting so you could fantasize about touching young women. Although, in retrospect, that was probably shortsighted of me."

A chuckle ran through the group.

"The fact is, not a single young woman has asked to audition for the squad as of yet. I just need to know what to expect if and when that happens. Will I lose any of you?"

The squad looked around the room in silence, wondering who would speak first. After thirty seconds had passed, Holway Manning II, who went by Holly, raised his hand.

"Sorry, Coach, but I think I'd have to quit."

The coach nodded solemnly.

"I respect your decision, Holly. I hope it won't come to that."

The coach was probably the only one who felt that way. Holly had earned the bemused scorn of his colleagues by being way too into cheerleading. His legacy went back to the days when "Boola Boola" was fresh out of the composer's head and he had made it his mission in life to restore the Yale Long Cheer, a quest no one else supported, especially after they'd heard it.

Marty raised his hand.

"Maybe, at first, at least, we could just sort of cheer side by side? Or take turns?"

"Afraid to lose your main squeeze, Langley?"

"What? No!"

Mason seemed energized by this line of thought. "My routine partners change. But you and Leighton are always paired off. Why is that?"

Marty felt his cheeks flush. "We don't make our own assignments," he said sheepishly.

"I'll take responsibility for that one, Mason," said the coach. "They're a perfect physical match for each other. That's why I keep them paired."

A couple of guys guffawed.

"A perfect physical match."

Widespread laughter was silenced abruptly by the coach's expression. "None of that, now. Anyone got anything useful to say?"

Everyone stared at the coach in silence.

"OK, then, let's do this. Let's help our guys leave Dirtmouth in the dust."

"Coach!"

"You didn't hear that."

+   +   +

Marty and Leighton sat side by side on the bus back to campus. Marty stared out the window, preoccupied.

"What's eating you?"

Reluctantly, Marty turned away from the window, but he didn't look at Leighton. "I guess the...the stuff the guys said."

"What stuff?"

Marty whipped his head toward Leighton.

"What do you mean, *what* comments? About you and me. Being some kind of item or something."

"What? You can't be serious!! Mason Deering is a jerk. Just forget about it."

Unfortunately, Marty was not sure he could do that.

They got off the bus at York and Broadway, in the heart of what passed for a shopping district in New Haven. Leighton wanted Marty's advice on a corsage for his date for the post-game dance; Marty's parents owned a florist's shop where he worked in the summers.

"It's gotta wow her, you know? Without being... tastelessly large or something. I'm hoping she's gonna give it up for me that night."

Marty wasn't sure a corsage could lead to intercourse, but kept that opinion to himself. "I do have a few questions," he said.

"OK, shoot."

"What color is her hair?"

"Sort of reddish-brownish-blondish."

"Great. That's very helpful. And her eyes?"

"Green. I think. Maybe brown. Or blue."

"Again, huge help. And what color will her dress be?"

"Geez, Marty, how the hell would I know that? I'll find out when I pick her up."

"Thoughtful gentlemen ask ahead of time," Marty said primly; he was able to answer all of his questions about his own date with ease.

They went into the florist and he ordered a spray of viburnum, lily of the valley and forget-me-nots for Sheila, who had accidentally-on-purpose let slip that her dress would be dark blue, sparing Marty the trouble of inquiring. For Leighton's date he picked a jaunty mix of ranunculi in three jewel tones highlighted by soft blue bachelor buttons, a combination Marty was pretty sure would go with any dress she ended up wearing.

"Who *are* you taking, anyway?" Marty asked as they paid for the flowers.

"Only the hottest woman at Wellesley. Her name's Sarah Messing. We've been out two times now, the Governors' Ball and then her Homecoming. She let me put my hand up her skirt when we made out after Homecoming, so I'm betting third time's the charm."

"How come you've never mentioned her?"

"I don't tell you *everything*. I suppose you're taking Sheila?"

"I am."

"You two ought to get married. You're already boring each other to death."

"Thanks a lot!" Marty said, chuckling in spite of himself. Sheila, an education major at Quinnipiac, was his reliable go-to date for special events, though they rarely saw one another in between, an arrangement that suited them both just fine.

Marty and Leighton walked back to the college and ate dinner in the dining hall, then went their separate ways at the library to study, or, in Leighton's case, nap. The overstuffed leather armchairs in the reading room got the best of him every time. Marty remained wide awake in a study carrel on the third floor, rousing Leighton shortly before the library closed at 10:00. When they got back to Branford their suite mates had gathered in the common room for the nightly ritual of watching The Dick Cavett show.

"Who's on?" Leighton asked as he and Marty came through the door.

"Queers, apparently. TV Guide calls them 'Stonewall activists.'"

Marty's roommate Mitchell emerged from their bedroom with a bowl of chocolate pudding he'd spirited from the dining hall. "Stonewall Jackson? He was queer?"

"No, not the general. It's some kind of drag bar in New York that got raided last June. The queers fought the police for two nights. Don't you read the newspapers?"

"Nope," said Mitchell, sucking pudding off his spoon with relish. "The profs give me more than enough to keep me busy."

In spite of being the first nighttime talk show host to interview homosexuals, Cavett was his usual sardonic self, cracking jokes in the monologue about everything but the subject of that night's show. When the "Stonewall activists" came on, they looked pretty ordinary.

"Really? These guys are queer?"

"Must have butched them up for the show."

"Shhh!"

"Sorry."

The room was quiet until Cavett asked about the relationship between two of the men opposite him.

"So, I understand that you and Mr. Evans here are...what word do you prefer?"

The man to whom the question was addressed turned and looked at the man to his right, then turned back to Cavett.

"We're lovers."

The audience in the studio as well as the Branford common room went up for grabs as Cavett's guests sat with impassive expressions on their faces amid the catcalls and boos. Cavett was able to shush his audience but had no power over his viewers.

"Holy shit! I can't believe he just said that!"

"*Lovers!* What does that even mean when it's two guys? What do they do?"

"Why, are you hoping to find out?"

Leighton rose from his chair and headed to the refrigerator, shaking his head. "Why don't you turn that shit off?" he asked, adding "Who wants beer?"

"Do *not* turn it off," said Barry, speaking for the first time since they'd sat down. "I want to listen."

"Really? Why?"

"Well, what if I said I thought I might be gay?"

"Tell us something we don't already know."

"Fuck you! Fuck you and shut up."

They watched the rest of the show in sullen silence. Barry's admission, if that's what it was, had taken all the fun out of it. Mitchell, who was sitting next to Barry, slowly eased his way farther down the sofa, hoping he wasn't being too obvious. No one seemed to notice that Marty hadn't volunteered an opinion.

When the show was over the beer-drinking began in earnest and the pall lifted.

"That was disgusting," said Mitchell. "Is this what we have to look forward to? Faggots everywhere?"

Barry cleared his throat by way of a reminder.

"What?" Mitchell went on. "You didn't actually mean that, did you? I thought you just wanted to hear the program."

"Maybe I did and maybe I didn't. It's my business, anyway."

An uncomfortable silence fell over the room once more as the suite mates contemplated the possibility of a queer in their midst.

Carl looked at Marty and Leighton. "What about you cheerleaders? You guys are all up in each other's crotches and everything."

"I beg your pardon?" said Leighton, using his frostiest aristocratic tone.

"Carl's right," said Donald. "Don't you see? Before all these Dick Cavett shows and whatnot, it seemed a little different. But now...all that hopping around in your tight white sweaters and pleated pants. Not to mention jumping into each other's arms..."

Marty and Leighton turned to one another, uncertain of how to defend themselves. Marty came up with a retort first. "The quarterback sticking his hands under the center's butt doesn't look too good, either, does it?"

Donald frowned. "Let's leave the quarterback out of it, OK?"

Marty took a swig of beer, pleased he'd shut Donald up.

+   +   +

It was one in the morning and Marty lay wide awake, replaying the day's events in an endless loop. Mitchell's snoring didn't help. He'd tried diligently for hours to block

Leighton out of his thoughts, but in the bleakness of the pitch-dark room he finally gave up. The fact is, he thought about Leighton every night, but after the cracks at the cheerleaders' meeting and the conversation tonight he realized his thoughts had a name, and that name scared the shit out of him.

Just the same, once he let it in the fantasy started as it always did, with Leighton using the springboard to leap high in the air, spread his legs in a split, then close them quickly and come down to the ground assisted by Marty's hands on his waist. Marty waited for that moment when his fingers slid under Leighton's sweater to his belt and then his shirt, where he could feel the moist skin of his flanks through the Oxford cloth. It only lasted a few seconds, but here in bed Marty could prolong the memory and enlarge upon it, sliding his hands higher up Leighton's sides as Leighton leaned back against him, his thick black hair brushing Marty's face and his butt pressed firmly against Marty's groin. With his hands circling Leighton's waist underneath his sweater, Marty began to kiss the back of his neck, then his ear, slowly and lovingly. The fantasy never got beyond that point because by then he would have to go to the bathroom and clean himself off, hoping the creak of the floor boards didn't wake Mitchell up.

It was the same tonight, except that after his climax Marty began to sob uncontrollably.

+   +   +

The next morning Marty paced up and down outside the chaplain's office, too nervous to knock on the door. William Sloane Coffin was a larger-than-life figure, nationally known—and widely despised—for his outspoken criticism of the war, but that wasn't what made Marty hesitate. As a choir member he'd had plenty of conversations with the chaplain before and after worship, and found him approachable and a good listener. Marty just wasn't sure he could get the words out for him to listen to.

"This is ridiculous," he finally muttered. He went to the office door and knocked on it, causing it to swing inward.

"Uh, Rev. Coffin?"

The chaplain swiveled his chair around to face the door.

"Bill, please. What's up, Marty?"

"I...I'm really worried about something. I...don't know what to do about it."

"Well, come on in and have a seat. Shut the door if you want."

Sloane Coffin looked more like a city editor than a clergyman, his white shirt sleeves rolled to the elbow and his tie loose at his neck. He put his cigarette out in the ashtray on the desk and leaned in toward Marty.

"Is it the draft? If you lost your exemption I can help you with that. We're mounting a court challenge next week..."

"No, it's not the draft."

"Oh." Sloane Coffin sat back again, waiting for Marty to speak.

Marty looked glumly at the floor, tapping his fingers nervously on the notebook in his lap. "I think I might be...be..." He couldn't finish the sentence. He jumped up and headed for the door. "I'm sorry to have bothered you."

"Marty, wait a second. That...last word, the one you couldn't say. Would that be 'gay' by any chance?"

Marty rested his forehead against the heavy oak door, listening to his breath.

"Maybe." Why had he come here? "Yes."

"Sit down."

Marty returned to his chair slowly, like a man walking to his execution.

"It's OK, you know. There are a lot of people will tell you it's not OK. But I'm not one of them."

Marty felt like he was going to cry.

"The world is changing. People who haven't spoken up for themselves are starting to speak very loudly. In twenty years you won't believe you and I had this conversation."

Marty didn't care about twenty years. He wondered how he'd get through tomorrow.

"Is there someone...special...that's made you think about this?"

Marty was silent, looking at the floor. At last he muttered: "My suite mate. Leighton."

"Leighton." The reverend rolled the name slowly off his tongue. "He's a very nice-looking guy. And a good human being. I think you should tell him how you feel."

This conversation was going way too fast for Marty. "I...I...I could never do that. I know he doesn't feel the same. It would ruin our friendship."

The chaplain looked at him calmly. The overhead light reflected off the huge lenses of his eyeglasses, making it hard for Marty to read his expression.

"Are you sure about that?"

Wait, Marty thought, did he know something about Leighton? How was that possible? Was he some kind of expert on who was gay? Marty's mind was racing and he couldn't sit still any longer. "Look, Rev... Bill, I mean. I really appreciate this talk, but I need to get going. I'll be late for class.

"OK, Marty," Bill said quietly. "See you in church."

+   +   +

Despite his initial reaction, Marty couldn't stop thinking about the chaplain's words. *I think you should tell him.* He was pretty sure he'd end up with a black eye, but he was sick of agonizing about it.

He found Leighton in his usual chair in the library, awake for once and reading a book.

"I got us a dinner reservation at Mory's tonight."

"Really? Mory's? You just get your assistance check or something?"

God, Leighton could still be such an asshole sometimes. Marty let out a frustrated sigh. "No," he said. "I just thought it might be fun. You know, before all the craziness starts tomorrow."

Leighton closed his book and stood up. "Sounds more like a special occasion to me. What am I forgetting?" He leaned in toward Marty's ear with a mischievous grin. "It's not our anniversary, is it, dear?"

Marty frowned and pulled his head away. Maybe this dinner wasn't such a great idea after all. "Talk about looking a gift horse in the mouth."

"Sorry, sorry. What time?"

"Seven."

"Great!"

They stood staring at each other, suddenly at a loss for words. Leighton looked down at the book in his hands.

"I'd better get back to this. I was supposed to have read it two weeks ago."

"OK, you do that. Try not to get a brain cramp from the exertion."

"Ha ha."

Marty decided he needed a new tie for dinner. He headed across campus to J. Press, where he found a great one, mint green with a red and white rep stripe. With a white button-down and a navy blazer it would look pretty snazzy. But when it came time to put it on that night, his hands were trembling so much he couldn't tie it. After four attempts he gave up, shoved his hands in his pockets and went to Leighton's room. Leighton was tying his own tie in front of the dresser mirror.

"A little help?" Marty said from the doorway. Leighton tugged on the points of his tie a final time and then turned to Marty.

"Really? You wear bow ties all the time. What's up?"

"Beats me. This one won't cooperate."

"OK, whatever."

Leighton planted himself in front of Marty and began whipping the two lengths of the tie over, around and under until a nice bow emerged. Marty tried not to laugh at the way Leighton stuck his tongue out while he worked.

"There," he said, pulling on the ends to tighten the knot. "You're a knockout. Sheila's gonna have to fill up your dance card fast tomorrow night before a bunch of other girls grab you."

Leighton dropped his hands to his side but didn't move away. They looked at each other in silence for three, four, five seconds. Marty spoke first.

"Silly Rabbit, boys don't have dance cards."

Leighton scowled and shook his head.

"What?" asked Marty.

"What d'you mean, *what*?" Leighton turned and grabbed his blazer off the bed.

"The way you were looking at me. Do I have toothpaste on my face or something?"

"You're imagining things. Let's go."

Marty was grateful when they were shown to a booth. The high wooden walls on either side of them would guarantee privacy, and privacy had never been a higher priority for him than tonight. They placed their order and handed the menus back to the waiter, then folded their hands on the table in identical poses.

"Leighton..."

"Really? 'Leighton'? You never call me by my first name."

"I don't?" Marty looked confused.

"No. This must be a special occasion after all. It *is* our anniversary, isn't it?" Leighton flashed the same mischievous grin again.

"How about 'Asshole'? Could I call you that?"

"Sorry. Please, Martin, say what you were going to say. I can't wait. '*Leighton*,'" he chuckled, shaking his head.

This wasn't how Marty had envisioned the conversation going. He had some notes in his shirt pocket, but if Leighton thought that using his first name was a laugh riot, he'd never let Marty live down referring to notes. Assuming, of course, they were still speaking after tonight.

"OK, here it is..." Marty took a gulp of air. "I've been— "

The sound of men's voices singing in close harmony cut him off in mid-sentence.

I love coffee, I love tea
I love the Java Jive and it loves me
Coffee and tea and the java and me
A cup, a cup, a cup, a cup, a cup

"*Really?*" Marty said. "The Whiffenpoofs?"

"It's 'cause of the game tomorrow. Lots of old timers in town."

"Oh."

The music got louder as the group approached their table. The men were snapping their fingers along with the song now. As they strolled past Marty and Leighton they nodded and smiled, singing the whole time.

"They're so fucking self-satisfied," Marty said once they'd passed by.

"Marty? Are you OK? Why are you in such a bad mood?"

He wanted to say Because I'm so in love with you I think I could die of it, and I only figured that out yesterday, but the waiter had returned with their food.

Mory's wasn't all that big, and soon the Whiffs were making a return trip.

He gave her kisses and promised the moon
But now he's singin' a different tune.
He left her waitin' alone at the church
He left her waitin' alone in the lurch
With all of her broken dreams it's no surprise
The sunshine girl has raindrops in her eyes.

Leighton was tucking into his lobster roll with gusto, while Marty's remained untouched. They're never going to shut up, Marty thought. I'll just have to make the best of it.

"I want to talk about our relationship," Marty said, slowly and loudly. Leighton showed no signs of hearing him. Marty rapped his fist on the table. Leighton looked up, startled.

"I SAID, I WANT TO TALK ABOUT OUR RELATIONSHIP."

It was like talking to a deaf person. The Whiffs had been hailed by a table of former members a few feet away who kept requesting more songs, so they had basically taken up residence in the room where Marty and Leighton were eating. All the other diners seemed delighted, resting their silverware on their plates to listen.

"I'M STARTING TO FEEL LIKE I HAVEN'T BEEN ENTIRELY HONEST WITH YOU," Marty practically shouted. Christ, they could probably hear him in Old Lyme...why couldn't Leighton hear him across the table?

> Bright College years, with pleasure rife,
> The shortest, gladdest years of life;
> How swiftly are ye gliding by!
> Oh, why doth time so quickly fly?
> The seasons come, the seasons go,
> The earth is green or white with snow,
> But time and change shall naught avail
> To break the friendships formed at Yale.

The table of alums was singing along now, loudly and drunkenly. Marty wanted to cry with frustration.

"HAVE YOU EVER THOUGHT WE MIGHT BE MORE THAN FRIENDS?"

Leighton peered at him, his face scrunched with the effort to read Marty's lips. It was no use. He put a hand to his ear and shook his head while he scooped up the last french fry with his other one. All at once, the music stopped. The Whiffs had moved to another room. Leighton looked at Marty's untouched plate.

"Aren't you going to eat that?"

"Naw, I'm really not hungry."

"Can I have it?"

"Sure."

Marty shoved his plate across the table with a little too much force.

Leighton looked at him quizzically. "Are you mad about something? At me?"

"What? No, of course not. I just thought...I thought we'd be able to talk over dinner, that's all."

Leighton, who normally had perfect table manners, seemed obsessed with his second lobster roll, practically shoving it into his mouth.

"It's quiet now," he observed when he finally took a breath between bites. "God, this is good. I'm sorry you lost your appetite. I, obviously, did not. What did you want to talk about?"

"It doesn't matter. It just that it's our last year at Yale and I wanted to celebrate that...celebrate you and...our friendship, I guess."

Leighton wiped his mouth and looked at Marty. "You're not going soft on me, are you?"

Marty didn't know what to say.

"You know how I feel about sticky sweet stuff," Leighton went on. "Especially from another guy."

"Yeah, I know. I just wanted to say it."

Leighton smiled at him.

"OK, well, thanks for saying it. And thanks for dinner."

The Whiffenpoofs had returned just long enough for their signature closer. The table of alums appeared to have slipped into an alcoholic stupor.

> *We are poor little lambs*
> *Who have lost our way.*
> *Baa! Baa! Baa!*
> *We are little black sheep*
> *Who have gone astray.*
> *Baa! Baa! Baa!*
> *Gentlemen songsters off on a spree*
> *Damned from here to eternity*
> *God have mercy on such as we.*
> *Baa! Baa! Baa!*

+   +   +

When Marty and Leighton got to the changing room at the Bowl they could hear Holly practicing the Long Cheer in the bathroom.

"Brekekekex, ko-ax, ko-ax! Brekekekex, ko-ax, ko-ax! O-OP, o-OP!"

"Does he *never* give it a rest?" Leighton asked no one in particular. "Hey, Manning!" he yelled, rapping on the bathroom door. "Get out of the can. Some of us need it for legitimate purposes."

Holly threw open the door and glared at Leighton.

"As if restoring the Long Cheer were not a legitimate purpose! But how could you understand? Doesn't your entire legacy consist of your father and grandfather? You don't have Yale in your blood."

"Well, excuse *me*, Thurston Howell IV. Don't tell me...your dad calls your mom 'Lovey,' doesn't he?"

"He certainly does not."

"Poopsy, then."

"*Nooo*," Holly sneered.

"Mummy?"

Holly blushed.

"Really."

The squad filed in one by one, exchanging Madras and pinstripe shirts and khaki pants for pristine white slacks, white button-down shirts, and form-fitting white sweaters with giant navy Ys sewn across their fronts. Last came the white socks and white bucks. Given the rough-and-tumble nature of what they were about to do, the squad's uniforms were not the most practical choice, but the boys prided themselves on hitting the field looking perfect, however they might look by the game's conclusion.

The coach arrived last, dressed identically to the squad, and gave them his usual pep talk, which everyone listened to with glazed eyes. The only motivation they needed was sitting out there in those stands, thousands upon thousands of them, and no words of encouragement could take the place of the adrenalin rush of making that many people sing and shout their lungs out.

The teams were being introduced over the loudspeaker now to polite applause. Next came the Dartmouth cheerleaders, and then it was their turn. They trotted up the ramp from the changing room to the field and received a hero's welcome, at least from the Elis. The squad smiled and waved and soaked in the adulation.

Each cheering squad got to lead a warm-up number to get people in the mood. A few boos greeted the Dartmouth team, but once they started the crowd singing "As the Backs Go Tearing By" the boos were soon drowned out by the sizeable number of Dartmouth fans in the crowd. Their singing sounded especially strident this year; everybody knew Dartmouth was favored to win, even if you couldn't find anyone in New Haven who would admit to that. The Yale squad took the field next, leading their own fans in the song they always started with.

Boola, Boola; Boola, Boola; Boola, Boola, Boola Boola!
When we roughhouse poor old Dartmouth,
They will holler Boola Boo.
Oh! Yale, Eli Yale!

The New Haven fans swayed back and forth jauntily, punctuating the final lines with little calf-raises along with the cheerleaders. When the song was over the squad leapt in the air randomly and clapped their hands as they exited the field and the game began.

True to the predictions, Yale stumbled in the first half, retiring from the field at a 21-7 disadvantage. The cheer squad would have their work cut out for them in the second half. Tumbling back into the changing room, they gulped ice water and wrapped cold towels around their necks; in spite of the brisk autumn weather they were soaked in sweat. As they cooled themselves off they waited for the sounds of the marching band to fill the air, but nothing happened.

"Why hasn't the band taken the field, Coach?" Leighton asked.

"I don't know," he replied. "I'll go and see."

The coach arrived at the top of the ramp just in time to hear an announcement come over the loudspeaker.

"Ladies and gentlemen, we have a special treat for you this afternoon. Please welcome senior Yale cheerleader Holway Manning II and members of the Yale classes of 1924, 1925 and 1928 to perform the historic Long Cheer!"

"That little shit!" the coach hissed under his breath. The squad had come up the ramp behind him, crowding around to see what was up.

Holly ran energetically to the fifty-yard line, followed closely by a group of about ten men in their late sixties wearing various versions of a Yale sweatshirt over loudly colored pants. He nodded his head three times and his group literally leapt into action.

First, they jumped in the air with surprising coordination and turned to their right in midair, landing as a unit and dropping to their right knees.

"*BREKEKEKEX, KO-AX, KO-AX!*" they shouted, pumping their elbows back and forth, then jumped in the air again and repeated the move to their left.

"*BREKEKEKEX, KO-AX, KO-AX!*"

Now they turned front and center.

"*O-OP! O-OP!*" they shouted, swinging their fists right and left.

"*PARABALOU! YALE! YALE! YALE!*

Then it was *RAH! RAH! RAH!* to the right, *RAH! RAH, RAH!* to the left, *RAH! RAH! RAH!* front and center before their big, loud finish.

"*YALE!*" (pause) "*YALE!*" (pause) "*YALE!*"

At that Holly and his geezers went to town, leaping and swiping their fists through the air like the Long Cheer was some kind of elixir of youth. The crowd roared its approval.

"You've just witnessed history, ladies and gentlemen!" boomed the announcer. "Perhaps it's time to bring the Long Cheer back to Yale!" The stands went crazy at this suggestion. "BRING...IT... BACK! BRING...IT... BACK!" they began chanting in unison, rising and stomping their feet for emphasis.

Coach Robins looked apoplectic. The squad had never seen him angry at all, let alone so angry he could wring a certain cheerleader's neck.

"Coach, do you think...?"

Marty's voice trailed off as he caught sight of the coach's expression.

"I thought we were in a competition with the Dartmouth squad today, but apparently we've been bested by our own side."

Robins stared at the ground for a moment, then looked at the squad.

"We're doing the 'Flying Y'," he announced.

Now it was the team's turn to look apoplectic.

"The 'Flying Y'? But, Coach, we never get it right!"

The coach looked grim.

"Well, you're going to get it right today. I want that crowd back!"

It was at that moment the boys realized their coach didn't give a shit about who won the football game.

"Cooper, Mason, Brodie, Xander, Ralph, Charlie and Tim, you're the bases."

"Right, Coach," Brodie said.

"Mike and Tommy, you spot."

"Got it."

There was only one assignment left, and it was a doozy.

"Leighton and Marty, you're the flyers."

Marty gulped.

"Uh..."

Robins glared at him.

"Yes?"

"Um, nothing, Coach."

"What about me, Coach?"

Everyone turned and looked at Holly leaning against the door to the changing room, a self-satisfied grin on his face.

"You won't be needed for this routine, Manning," Robins said, crossing the room at a brisk pace and brushing past Holly as he went through the door. "Or for any subsequent routines."

The grin disappeared from Holly's face.

The squad filed out of the room, most of them ignoring Holly.

"Well, what the hell did you expect, Manning?" Leighton asked as he got to the door. "You made a fool out of Robins."

"Besides," Mason added, "you said you were quitting anyway."

They waited for a response but Holly only looked at the ground, silent. Marty suddenly felt sorry for him. The guy had pulled off a major stunt today, after all, even if his mode of execution was badly chosen. Marty was the last to leave the room, so he leaned in to speak in Holly's ear.

"It was *amazing.*"

Holly raised his head and Marty saw a tear glistening in his left eye. He gripped Marty's upper arm and squeezed.

"Thank you," he mouthed, his voice stuck in his throat.

The team ran onto the field just as the marching band was leaving. They saw Coach intercept the drum major and speak intently with him, making emphatic gestures with his hands as the two men put their heads together. The drum major nodded and went to tell the band about the change in plans.

By the end of the third quarter Yale was trailing 35-14, and unless Eli Yale had a miracle to send the team's way from the ether the outcome was clear to everyone in the stands. People had begun to leave, turning their sights to the evening's festivities. From Coach Robins's point of view, the set-up was perfect, because no one from Yale cared about the football game anymore but they could still root for the best cheerleading squad in New England. He'd sent a note to the announcer. As the players ran off the field his voice boomed out over the band music.

"Ladies and gentlemen, this is a big day for Yale cheerleaders! You've already witnessed the return of the Long Cheer, a bit of Yale history. Now you are about to witness, for the first time ever, what may be the hardest routine ever undertaken by our Boys Who Make the Noise. Please welcome back the Yale Cheerleaders and the first-ever performance of..."

A drum roll sounded from the band as the squad ran on to the field.

"THE FLYING 'Y'!"

Fans who had been gathering their coats and standing up to leave sat down again, and those already at the exits turned back. Coach had decided they'd combine the routine with Cole Porter's "Bull-Dog," always a crowd favorite. The squad lined up facing the stands and led the singing while the band thundered the accompaniment. The words sounded ironic in light of the score, but the zippy music lifted the fans' mood.

> *Bull-DOG! Bull-DOG! Bow, wow, wow!*
> *Eli Yale!*
> *Bull-DOG! Bull-DOG! Bow, wow, wow!*
> *Our team can never fail!*
> *When the sons of Eli break through the line,*
> *That is the sign we hail!*
> *Bull-DOG! Bull-DOG!*
> *Bow, wow, wow!*
> *Eli Yale!*

Normally the team would jump in the air and clap to end the song, but as another drum roll began they turned and ran single file into the middle of the field, then turned and faced the stands again. The spotters took places opposite each other and dropped to one knee. The drum roll got louder as, one at a time, the bases ran between the spotters, somersaulted, and came up in a headstand. It would be extremely easy for the newest addition to send the others tumbling like dominoes, so the spotters had their work cut out for them. When all seven of the bases had lined up in close formation, they spread their legs in unison to form a living corridor of the letter Y. Raucous applause burst from the crowd as Marty and Leighton prepared for the big finish.

Marty muttered a quick prayer. There was no room for error.

He nodded in the direction of the band and the drum roll stopped. An eerie silence descended on the field, which Marty broke with a yell that masked his terror:

"ELI!" he shouted, and ran toward the canyon of spread legs.

And as he got close it was like God was whispering in his ear: *Jump...NOW!*

Marty leapt with all his might, his arms extended in front of him like a diver's, and the next thing he knew he was out the other side of the formation, tucking his head and somersaulting into a standing position. Dumbstruck, the crowd forgot to applaud.

Then Leighton shouted "YALE!" and repeated Marty's leap without a hitch, coming up right beside him. The bases pushed up and out of their headstands one after the other and joined the happy flyers, relieved beyond words that their reproductive capabilities had not been compromised.

The fans went wild.

"AGAIN!" they screamed, "AGAIN!"

Coach Robins had joined his squad on the field, smiling and waving as he muttered "Don't even think about it," under his breath. Then, in a gentler tone, he added: "Why mess with perfection?"

While they basked in the crowd's appreciation the squad members were clapping Marty and Leighton on the back and shaking their hands.

"The men of the hour!" said Cooper, grinning broadly.

Leighton tossed his head back over his shoulder to look at Marty, beamed, and threw an arm in his direction.

"We did it, sport!"

Marty grasped his hand and squeezed it hard; then the squad engulfed them as the crowd rose to its feet and cheered.

"Coach was right," Mason said in Leighton's ear in a low but perfectly audible tone. "You two are perfectly matched."

Leighton and Marty turned as one to look at Mason, who cast his eyes down to their still-clasped hands.

Leighton abruptly let go of Marty's hand and shoved him by the shoulder so that he fell against a startled Xander. He just had time to see the stunned look on Marty's face before he repositioned himself on the other side of Cooper and resumed waving to the crowd as though nothing had happened. Marty didn't feel like waving anymore, so he ran to the changing room slightly ahead of the squad, determined not to cry.

On the bus back to campus Leighton sat as far from Marty as he could.

+   +   +

Leighton holed up in his room while everybody dressed for the dance. Marty tied his black tie without any help, but with little enthusiasm for the evening's activities.

The flowers had been delivered to their suite and as he picked up Sheila's corsage he looked sadly at the one he'd designed for Leighton's date, remembering better times.

"Fuck Dick Cavett," he muttered under his breath. "He ruined my goddam life."

The Commons was a vision of soft light and flowers, all of them blue or white. Linen tablecloths and napkins transformed the wooden cafeteria tables into a reasonable facsimile of a first-class restaurant. They were arranged around the periphery of the room, creating a generous dance floor in the center.

Marty didn't feel like drinking. He told Sheila he'd get them two rum and Cokes, but only Sheila's had rum in it. She took modest little sips from her glass as they chatted about their classes and news of their families. Eventually she picked up on Marty's sadness. In a moment of silence between them she reached across the table and tapped him on the nose.

"You OK?"

Marty was surprised by the intimacy of her gesture, but not displeased. He needed to feel like someone cared about him tonight. He wasn't about to open up to her, but he didn't want to lie, either.

"Sorry it's so obvious. I've got a lot on my mind right now, and it's kind of got me down."

"Want to talk about it?"

"Definitely not." Marty's face lit up in a sudden smile. "See? All better now. Let's dance."

Moving around the floor actually did raise Marty's spirits. Sheila, who hadn't gone to the game that afternoon, was impressed by the number of people who came up to congratulate Marty on the Flying Y.

"So, where's your other half?" one of them asked, a question that made Marty stop dancing so abruptly that Sheila stepped on his foot.

"Ow! Excuse me?"

"The other guy that sailed through the formation. I don't know his name."

"Oh, Leighton? I'm not sure. Haven't seen him."

"Well, tell him we thought he was great, too."

"Sure. Will do."

After the well-wisher had moved away Marty realized he had not seen Leighton anywhere that evening. The room was packed, and in any case Leighton was probably avoiding him, but Marty was surprised he hadn't at least glimpsed him from a distance. God knows, the man would always stand out in a crowd.

In spite of Leighton's cruelty that afternoon, Marty began to worry about him. He asked everyone who knew them both whether they'd seen him, but no one had.

Something was definitely wrong.

He could tell that the growing anxiety in his voice was leading Sheila to put two and two together, so he escorted her back to her hotel and gave her a chaste peck on the cheek before she could test any theories. Then he ran all the way back to Branford, visions of Leighton dead on the floor of his room speeding his steps.

But Leighton was not dead on the floor of his room. The suite was empty.

Marty searched every corner of the suite before finally going into his own room and switching on the light between the beds. On his pillow sat the corsage for Leighton's date, still in its plastic container. Beneath it lay a stack of cocktail napkins covered in writing.

Marty lifted the flowers gently and put them to one side, then picked up the napkins. *Richter's, New Haven's Oldest Bar* was stamped in gold on them. The lengthy message was full of smears and scratch-outs, but it was definitely Leighton's handwriting.

Marty crossed to his desk and sat down heavily on the chair. He turned on the study lamp and started to read.

Dear Asshole,

I'm sorry to call you that but everything else I'm going to say is so sappy I have to do something to balance it. First of all, I'm sorry I was such a shit to you this afternoon. I deserve to lose your friendship forever but I hope I don't.

On the next napkin:

You see, I had a big revelation tonight. When I picked up Sarah's corsage, the one you had chosen, I realized I knew the color of your hair, and your eyes, and of every outfit you own without looking. Don't believe me? You wore a navy blazer, white shirt, and a mint green tie with red and white stripes to Mory's.

Then:

I could actually hear you perfectly well last night, in spite of the Whiffs. I had to pretend I couldn't because while I was tying your tie my knees started to shake, I was so gaga about being that close to you and touching your chin with my hands. Rev. Coffin said I should just tell you how I felt, but I thought you didn't feel the same until last night.

And another:

I'm sorry I didn't just talk to you right then and there. I only made a pig of myself with your lobster roll to keep from saying all the same things back to you that you were brave enough to say and I wasn't.

And:

I'm leaving the corsage for you because the colors go much better with your eyes and hair than Sarah's, especially since she's probably a uniform angry red right now after being stood up. I don't recommend you wear it, though, because people might think you're queer. Ha ha.

Followed by:

I'm taking the train home tonight to get my car and then I'm just going to drive and drive until I can clear my head a little. I hope while I'm gone you won't let your dance card get too filled up. In fact, dammit, just put my name on every line. Oh, I forgot. Boys don't have dance cards. You can probably tell I'm a little drunk right now.

And finally:

Geez, Marty, I'm not only drunk, I'm a complete mess, but I know one thing (here it comes). I love you. So much. Please bear with me. Please. While I — we— figure this out.

L.

P.S.: Upside. If they do start a draft lottery, this will definitely keep us out of Nam.

Marty took all the napkins and laid them in a row on his desk, smiling so hard he thought his face would break. He loosened his tie and took off his jacket. Then he stacked the napkins again and put them in a desk drawer along with the corsage, in case Mitchell came in. He grabbed his keys and headed out to the quad. The night had turned cold, but he didn't notice.

Marty had studied the carillon for a while but after he gave it up the teacher forgot to ask for his key to Harkness Tower back, so it was still on his ring. He opened the door as quietly as possible and began climbing, past the clock and the carillon, up the metal spiral staircase that begins after the stone steps end, right to the empty square room at the very top of the tower. The campus lay sprawled before him, its lights compartmented into a giant grid by the colleges, peaceful and perfect. Leaning against the stone frame of an arched window, Marty let himself go all soft inside, knowing Leighton would never have a goddamned thing to say about that ever again.

The Even More Miraculous Apostasy of (Now Just) Jeremy

It's been almost two years since Jeremy laid his hands on me in blessing and then smiled at me. I swore I'd carry that smile with me till I died, but the fact is the memory is already getting a little indistinct. I can go a whole morning or afternoon without even thinking about him now. Evenings are a little harder. There's no distraction from my students or the noise of the world going about its business. Sometimes the bottle helps, and sometimes it just makes it worse. But at least I've stopped crying myself to sleep. That was tedious.

When my parents read the letter dismissing me from seminary they got all hepped up about reparative therapy. I'd lived a pretty sheltered existence up till then but even I knew that was cruel and unusual punishment, not to mention a waste of time. I had *loved* Jeremy with all my heart. I didn't want to be cured of that. And, for God's sake, I was twenty-seven years old. They pretty much said "Well, have a good life" after that and I said "OK, I will," but this past Christmas I got a nice sweater with a card signed "Love, Mom and Dad," so we'll see.

I've crossed church off the list. I miss the Mass, but the traditionalist Catholic network is such a rumor mill I knew there'd be finger-pointing no matter where in the Northwest I went to church. Maybe even a priest refusing me communion. I did screw up my courage one day to attend a *Novus Ordo* Mass, my first. We sang a song that involved clapping in place of the *Gloria in excelsis* and then held hands during the Our Father. I headed for the door before communion. Sunday mornings have become a great time for a long run.

By all accounts, Seattle is a fantastic place to be gay, but I haven't really taken advantage of that yet. I'm still learning to say the words "I" and "gay" in the same sentence. I did put in an appearance at a couple of bars, but they were scarier than the *Novus Ordo* Mass. The false intimacy was exactly the same. I guess I should be grateful that more than one great-looking guy gave me his number, but none of them seemed interested in conversation, just sex. I don't miss sex. I miss Jeremy.

Figuring out a wardrobe was another challenge. I'd worn a black cassock every day since I was eighteen, and before that a uniform at the Academy. It became really obvious to me that regular people use their clothes to make some kind of statement, but I had no idea what mine should be. "Disgraced seminarian" didn't immediately suggest fashion choices, so I went with your basic khakis and button-down shirts for school, and jeans and hoodies on the weekends until I started to notice what other guys my age were wearing and began to cultivate some kind of taste. It made me feel like Rip Van Winkle, waking up after a hundred-year nap.

I've made friends with a lot of the teachers at my school, and they're really good about including me in social stuff, even family outings, so I don't feel lonely, though apart from that I'm by myself most of the time. My spiritual director at the seminary thought I was cut out to be a monastic; maybe he was right. A secular monk, of course. But I want to be a monk by choice, not default. I can definitely see the novelty of living alone wearing off.

+   +   +

I listen to some jazz while I clean up my dishes. I'm a pretty good cook these days, though I have to be careful about my weight now that I can eat whatever I want. Our food was strictly portioned at the seminary, and we had some kind of manual labor and some kind of exercise built into every day, so nobody ever needed to have his cassock let out. Frankly, I miss the regulated life, but the Sockeye salmon with Béarnaise sauce I made for dinner is a pretty decent trade-off. The closest thing we'd have gotten in seminary would have been crab cakes with ketchup.

Soon it's time to turn out the lights. Just as I close my bedroom door, I hear the intercom buzz. One of my neighbors is being stalked by an ex-boyfriend who can't take "no" for an answer. He shows up at least once a week and buzzes every apartment in the building, hoping that someone will let him in by mistake. We've learned to be cautious because we all want to help her get rid of this creep. I know I'm not expecting anybody so I consider just letting it buzz away, but if it goes on too long it'll kill my pleasant sleepiness, so I decide to get rid of it.

"Yes?" I say, holding down the button. I wait for an answer. Nothing. Sure enough, must be the stalker. I head back to the bedroom. The thing buzzes again. This is getting annoying.

"*Yes?*" I'm trying to sound quietly fierce. Still nothing. This time I wait awhile.

OK then, off to bed.

It's like the guy can see into my apartment. He waits till I'm once again closing my bedroom door before buzzing a third time. Now I'm loaded for bear.

"*Look!*" I pretty much shout, pressing the button so hard my thumb turns white. "Linda wants nothing more to do with you! Do us all a favor and go home, OK?"

"Kevin?"

The voice is quiet and husky, like someone with a sore throat, and I'm not sure whether I actually heard my name.

"I'm sorry?"

"Kevin, it's me."

I begin shaking all over like a person with a fever standing in a cold room. My voice catches in my throat.

"I'm sorry, but who are you?"

"It's Jeremy."

This can't be happening. Jeremy has ascended to live with the saints. We do not inhabit the same earthly plane anymore. Each Mass he celebrates takes him farther out of this world, and he's said hundreds by now. It's some kind of mistake.

"I think you must be looking for some other Kevin," I hear myself say, though the odds of that are probably astronomical.

"Kevin, *stop*. Please. Let me come up to your apartment."

It's definitely Jeremy's voice, but not like I've ever heard it before. He sounds...*desperate*. And tired, too.

"Um...OK...I guess," not at all sure I want this. "Take the elevator to four and turn right. I'm 410."

I hold down the Enter button long enough to get him through the outer and inner doors, then pivot away from the intercom, flattening myself against the wall so I don't fall down. I feel like a deer caught in the crosshairs of a hunter's rifle. In just a moment a bullet will pierce my chest and strike me dead. I seem to have stopped breathing already.

I hear the elevator doors open and then close again. The hallway is carpeted, so I don't hear anything else until the knock on my door. It's a sad, hesitant little knock.

I open the door.

Jeremy is standing in the hallway.

My hallway.

Outside the door to my apartment.

In Seattle.

He's wearing a black pea coat over his black cassock and Roman collar. He must have turned some heads walking through this part of town, where ink and piercings are way more common than priests. He has a backpack thrown over his right shoulder.

I can't bear to look at him directly, so I glance at his nose, then down at his shoes, then settle on his hairline. Even this way I take in the dark circles under his dark eyes, his cheeks hollower than usual. Despite how I'm feeling, *he* looks like the hunted one.

I say words I never thought I would say to him again in this lifetime. "Come in."

I step out of the way and he walks past me, the chill of the February night trailing off his clothes. He lets the backpack slide from his shoulder to the floor and looks around at the darkened room.

"This is nice." He turns to me. "You look good," he says, wearily. "Great, actually," he adds, looking away, suddenly shy. I'm not ready for this conversation.

"What are you doing here?"

I look him in the eye for the first time, and he holds my gaze. He opens his mouth to speak, but the words don't come. He takes a gulp of air and swallows it. "I've left."

"Left what? Portland?"

"The Fraternity. The priesthood, too, I guess."

I fold my arms across my chest, defending myself against this news.

"You sure don't look like you've left. You're wearing a collar, and, if memory serves, no pants under that cassock. Must have been kind of an impulsive decision."

I hear the sound of my voice and I can tell my words are making some kind of sense but they're really just a smokescreen to hide the chaos that's filling my mind because *Jeremy* is standing in my *living* room, *talking* to me.

"It was and it wasn't. I've been thinking about it for, like, six months, but I didn't know it would be today until it was. Today, I mean." He looks at his backpack on the floor. "And I did bring pants. Can I sit down?"

"Sure," I say, mechanically. We'll just sit down. Sit down and *chat* about what's *new*. "Let me turn on some lights."

I'm glad to have some activity to mask my dis-ease. Jeremy takes off his coat and throws it on a chair. He's thinner than usual, too thin.

"Do you want something to drink? There's some white wine in the refrigerator, and I've got scotch."

"Yes, please."

"Which?"

"Scotch."

"OK."

I put some ice in two glasses and cover it with Dewar's. I hand a glass to Jeremy and nod toward the sofa. He sits, looking down at the drink cupped in his hands. I take a chair nearby, moving it several inches farther away from the sofa.

"So..."

My invitation gets no immediate response. The room is so quiet I can hear Jeremy breathing. Then, as though someone has flipped a switch inside him, he takes a gulp of his scotch and starts talking.

"It all started with the declaration of the Jubilee Year last December. The Pope published a letter saying that no one was excluded from the Year of Mercy, and that included the Fraternity, and because he wanted to be merciful to *us* he would declare our sacramental absolutions licit and valid, but only during this one year."

"Yeah, I saw that online."

"Well, that got me thinking. Were the absolutions I'd given before that *illicit* and *invalid*? What about the Masses I'd celebrated? Were they all just *fake* because we took our marbles and left the Church after Vatican II?"

"I don't get it. The pope's opinion has never mattered to you before. We were taught to believe he's wrong about everything."

"Yeah, well, I guess I started to question that. I went back and read all the documents, the ones that we were told prove we have supplied jurisdiction because a state of emergency exists in the church and that state justifies our orders..."

I have not missed the phrase "supplied jurisdiction" in my life, even for a moment, or any of the endless hair-splitting of canon law that the traditionalists use to prove they're right and the Vatican is wrong. In spite of the shock of having Jeremy right in front of me again, his passionate rehearsal of this shit is leaving me cold. I start to tune him out, just catching a *normae generales* here and "formal versus doctrinal schism" there while I'm really concentrating on my scotch, wondering where all this is going.

Jeremy has become more energized as he's unfolded his boring story. He stands up and starts to pace around the room. "Kevin, I started to worry that I might actually be endangering people's *souls*, leading them away from the truth even while I was insisting that we were upholding it together. And every day it just made me crazier and crazier—should I keep doing what I'm doing or break away? And that's when I decided to find you, to see what you would say."

He puts his drink down on the coffee table, and I sense some kind of announcement is coming.

"And there was another thing..."

He hesitates, picking at a piece of fuzz on the front of his cassock. Then he looks at me.

"I realized how much I missed you. I...I still love you, Kevin."

My fist connects with Jeremy's jaw at about ninety miles per hour, sending him reeling backwards across the room, over an ottoman and down onto the floor, where his head smacks the bottom of the front door really hard.

And I have only begun.

"You *love* me?" I scream at his crumpled body. "You cost me my vocation, you fucker! I could have been a priest, goddammit! A *priest*, instead of some piddly-shit junior high teacher!"

I can tell my neighbors are opening their doors, not sure they're hearing this right.

"You *lied* to the rector about us. You told him I *seduced* you. Oh, yeah? Who kissed who on that soccer field?

Hmm...wasn't it *Jeremy* who kissed *Kevin*? Wasn't it *Jeremy* who took the lead in all subsequent conjugal activity? Well? Wasn't it?"

Jeremy is feeling his jaw tentatively.

"Ow," he says, sounding more surprised than hurt.

"But the minute we got found out you just disowned me! Didn't you, asshole? Did you love me then? Huh?"

"Ow," he says again, checking the back of his scalp and finding it moist. "I think I'm bleeding."

"Ask me if I care. And now after screwing my life up six ways to Sunday you have the nerve to show up and tell me that you *love* me. Well, buddy, you and I must have different definitions of that word."

Jeremy is struggling to get up but his legs are tangled in his cassock and he keeps sitting back down, his arms flailing. It would be amusing if I weren't so angry.

"And another thing. If you think you can show up in my life again after radio silence for two years and tell me you love me at the tail end of a discourse on *canon law*, like an afterthought, for God's sake, you've got another think coming. At least have the decency to say that *first*."

Jeremy has finally found a way to get himself straightened up by using the front door knob. He rises shakily to his feet and looks at me pleadingly.

"I'm sorry, I'm sorry, you're right! It should have been the first thing out of my mouth. I had to get my courage up, I guess. Ow! It hurts to talk. You hit me really *hard*."

He clearly expects me to feel sorry for him but he's barking up the wrong tree.

"There's more where that came from, so I think you'd better go before you get your second helping."

"Go?" Jeremy looks dumbfounded. "You want me to go?"

"Yes, you heard me. Get the fuck out of my apartment."

To my utter amazement, Jeremy bursts into tears. I have never seen him cry and wouldn't have thought him capable.

"Please. *Please*, Kevin. Don't make me go. It was so hard to decide to come here. I know I've been a complete *shit* to you. No question about it, a complete shit, but the fact is, I'm just not as brave as you."

"What's that supposed to mean?"

"You mean everything to me. But when it came to a choice between you and being a priest I turned out to be completely spineless. I was so proud of you for the way you stood up to the rector, but I just couldn't do it, I couldn't. I thought I would die if I didn't become a priest. But what kind of a priest can I be if I needed to lie to get ordained?"

He takes a handkerchief out of the pocket of his cassock and wipes his face with it but dissolves in tears again as soon as it's dry.

"It was always about you. You're why I left. Not canon law. Of course not canon law."

Until this moment I had thought those words, if I were ever to hear them, would give my life back to me, but I feel absolutely nothing.

"I'm sorry, Jeremy, it's too late. I'm over you. I'm sorry. Just go. It was a mistake to come."

He stands there motionless, still crying, so I grab his shoulders and turn him around and shove him out the front door, slamming it behind him. Then I see his coat and backpack and gather them up, not because he'll need them but because I don't want them in my house. I toss them out into the hall and slam the door again.

My neighbors sure didn't need their premium cable channels tonight.

I pour what's left of Jeremy's scotch into my glass and walk to the big window in the living room. My funky neighborhood is alive with color and movement, people going into and out of the latest hot bars and restaurants, while in the distance the skyscrapers of Seattle glow with the never-ending work of cleaning crews.

As though waking from a dream, I set my glass down gently on a side table.

What the *fuck*?

What have I done? What was I thinking?

"Oh, God, Jeremy!"

In a panic, I throw open the door and dash into the—

"WHOA!" The hideous orange carpeting of the hallway rushes up to meet my face as I fall over Jeremy's seated body and land heavily on my chest, my legs waving stupidly in the air behind me.

"Ow!" I say, feeling my nose to see if it's broken.

"Serves you right," Jeremy says, though without much conviction.

I roll over on my side and look at him.

"Still here, I see."

"I was hoping you might change your mind."

I hear a squeak and look down the hall in time to see a neighbor spying on us through her barely open door.

"Let's go back inside," I say.

I get to my feet first and offer Jeremy a hand. When I pull him up our faces come close and it seems like he's going to kiss me, so I let go of his hand and head through the open door. I'm not ready for that. Not yet.

"C'mon, let's get a look at that head."

He follows me docilely into the bathroom and sits on the closed toilet lid. I make a spinning motion with my finger to indicate he should turn around and he obeys. Then I soak a wash cloth in warm water and dab at the wound on his crown. The blood has already dried and matted in his hair, which is good, because it means he's not still bleeding. I get the Bactine out of the medicine chest.

"This is going to sting, okay?"

Jeremy nods. I spray the antiseptic on the wound and he flinches but makes no sound. My brave boy. Stop thinking like that, Kevin. And by all means fight that urge you're feeling right now to smooth his hair and kiss the pain away. One step at a time.

"You're all set. Doesn't look too bad. How does it feel?"

"It aches, I guess. My jaw is worse."

"I'll put the aspirin on the counter."

I glance at the clock and see that it's almost midnight. I have class at eight in the morning. "We'd better turn in. Do you have something to sleep in or do you need some pajamas?"

"I have a night shirt."

Of course. I had forgotten about those.

"Okay, I'll fix up the sofa for you."

"Can't I sleep with you?"

"No."

"Why not?"

"Because until two hours ago I thought I wouldn't see you again until I died—if then. I don't know what I think about all this yet."

"You came looking for me after you threw me out. You brought me back inside."

"See previous comment. I've got an early class. I need my beauty rest."

"No," Jeremy says, looking up at me with the tiniest smile. "You don't."

I put a sheet, blanket, and pillow on the sofa while Jeremy takes his backpack into the bathroom to change. I'm suddenly bone tired, can't imagine why. I knock softly on the bathroom door.

"See you in the morning."

"Okay, good night," comes from the other side. I imagine him opening the door to try to give me a kiss, which I would refuse. I feel a little pissed when he doesn't.

+   +   +

In spite of the evening's drama I conk out as soon as my head hits the pillow and sleep soundly through the night, waking up just a few minutes before the alarm goes off. I get out of bed, throw on my robe, and head to the bathroom. It feels strange and wonderful to know that Jeremy is asleep in the living room.

Or at least I hope he is.

The room is pretty dark so it scares the shit out of me when my toe kicks something large at the foot of the bed that I know wasn't there last night. The hair on my arms stands up as I try to process what the hell I'm looking at. Oh, for God's sake—it's Jeremy. He brought his pillow and blanket into my bedroom during the night and slept curled up on the floor. It's such a sweet, sweet thing to do I want to wake him up and tell him I love him and everything will be OK, but I don't. I let him sleep. I gather up clothes for the day and tiptoe out the door.

When I come out of the bathroom, dressed and ready for work, Jeremy is sitting at the kitchen table in his night shirt.

"What's for breakfast?"

"Uh, cereal is for breakfast."

"The housekeeper usually makes us scrambled eggs and sausages and grilled tomatoes. Sometimes French toast."

I retrieve a box of raisin bran from the cabinet and slap it on the table in front of Jeremy.

"You'll find milk in the 'refrigerator,'" I say, making sneer quotes with my fingers. "That's the big appliance over there. I use it to keep things cold. Just pull on the door handle to open it."

Jeremy scowls at my sarcasm but says nothing.

"I get home around six. I left my spare key for you on the counter over there, so you can come and go. I'll see you tonight, OK?"

Jeremy still says nothing, just sulks. My hand is already on the front door when, in spite of my best intentions, I come back and kiss the top of his head.

"I'm sorry. We'll do better tomorrow."

"Bye," he says.

I have a great day at school, buoyed by the knowledge that Jeremy is waiting at home for me. I don't tell anybody my happy secret because, really, how would I explain it? It would take hours. The new Kevin has a lot going for him, but now I realize the old Kevin did, too. I actually feel like a whole person today. I try and fail to put the brakes on my expectations.

I swing by Pike Place Market on my way home and pick up some gorgeous mussels, salad ingredients, and a baguette. I'm looking forward to impressing Jeremy with my culinary skills, but when I get off the elevator I smell cooking odors coming from inside the apartment.

I open the front door and see Jeremy moving around in the kitchen, an oven mitt on his hand.

"Hello!" I call.

He crouches down to look inside the oven.

"Welcome home," he says over his shoulder.

"Are you *cooking*?"

"Looks that way."

I come into the kitchen and put my grocery bags down on the counter. Jeremy looks at them a little sheepishly.

"I'm sorry! I should have known you'd get food, too. I just needed something to do."

"Listen, it's no problem! This is...a real treat. A surprise, I have to say, but a treat. No one has cooked for me since I moved here."

"Really? No one?" He brightens at this information.

"Nope, no one."

I finally take note of the fact that Jeremy's not wearing a cassock. For the past seven years I've only seen him in a cassock or naked, never in civvies. He's wearing black pants and loafers, a white button down shirt, and a blue V-neck sweater. The clothes fit him reasonably enough, but their complete lack of style screams "Catholic priest," even without the collar.

His jaw looks swollen and kind of purple and I immediately feel like a heel for having been the cause of that. It also reminds me that if I was that angry less than twenty-four hours ago, we probably still have a lot to talk about.

"So, what's on the menu?" I expect this is going to be a well-intentioned but hard-to-get-down meal. I'm already thinking of polite comments I can make.

"Uh, well, I made a Beef Wellington...that's what's in the oven, and I wrapped asparagus in some bacon...that'll go in when the roast comes out...and a mâche salad with poached pears. Didn't want the meal to get too heavy."

I stare at him in disbelief.

"What? Is there something wrong? You haven't become a vegetarian, have you?"

"When did you learn to cook? I've known you all my life and I don't remember you ever so much as putting a hot dog in a pot of boiling water."

He makes a scowly face and turns away. "For heaven's sake, Kevin. My family is in the restaurant business. We all cook."

Actually, his family has more like a restaurant empire, but it never occurred to me that meant they knew their way around a kitchen.

"Well, then, I'll set the table."

"Done."

"Oh." I put my head out into the dining room and see the table nicely set. A small vase of daffodils provides a startling burst of color.

"That's a great market you've got. I found everything I needed in one place."

I watch, fascinated, as he shuttles back and forth between the kitchen and dining room, putting the amazing-looking food on the table.

"Don't just stand there. Pour the wine. It's on the counter."

I fetch the bottle, a cabernet-shiraz blend with an unfamiliar label. It smells great as it tumbles into the glasses.

"Really, you know about wine, too?"

Jeremy just smiles and takes his seat. I join him and pick up my glass to propose a toast to the chef when Jeremy bows his head and makes the sign of the cross.

"*Benedic nos Domine et haec Tua dona ...*"

By reflex I join my voice to his.

"*...quae de Tua largitate sumus sumpturi. Per Christum Dominum nostrum. Amen.*"

I've said that prayer all my life but not once in the past two years. I feel it spread a chill over the table which I try to ignore by concentrating on the food.

"Oh, my God...Oh my *God*, Jeremy! This is fantastic!" I toss my rehearsed comments into the Recycle Bin and offer totally sincere praise for every part of the meal. Jeremy just nods as I gush, but I can tell he's pleased.

After fifteen minutes of non-stop eating I finally come up for air. "Whew! It's just...so damn good."

"I'm glad."

I put my knife and fork down for the first time since we started. "So. How did you manage to find me?"

He gives me a sidelong glance, which means the next thing out of his mouth will be a lie.

"The Internet, of course."

"You despise computers and don't know how to use them."

"I don't *despise* them. Not when they can be...helpful."

I stare at him until he looks me in the eye.

"OK, I had my mother do it for me."

"You *told* her about us?"

"What? No! I just said I wanted to visit you, see how you were. She still doesn't know why you left the seminary, or why you didn't get ordained."

"What did you tell her?"

"That you wanted some time off before you took the plunge, to travel, maybe sow a few wild oats."

"Oh, great! I'm sure she loved that."

"She did, actually. I think she's sorry I didn't do the same thing."

"If she only knew you're a veritable feedbag..."

"Yeah, if she only knew..." Jeremy's voice trails off, and his face looks sad all of a sudden. In the light of the table candles his jaw looks even worse. I reach out and touch it gently, but he recoils from even my light caress.

"I am so sorry, Jeremy. I don't know what came over me."

He takes a sip of his wine and looks at the glass meditatively.

"The way I see it, I had it coming."

The meal seems less festive now, and we finish it in silence.

"I'll do the dishes," I say, standing up. Jeremy stands, too, and pushes his chair under the table. Then, with his hands on the chair back, he starts to pray again.

"*Agimus tibi gratias, omnipotens Deus, pro universis beneficiis tuis, qui vivis et regnas in saecula saeculorum.*"

This time I just stand there with my plate in my hands, not reciting the prayer with him. If he notices, he doesn't say anything. When he's finished, I take all the plates I can manage out to the kitchen and start loading the dishwasher. I feel cross, like the prayers were some kind of bad magic. Bad for us, at least.

"You OK?" Jeremy has come into the kitchen holding the platter with the roast on it.

"Yeah, sure, why?"

"You got pretty quiet."

"I'm fine. The plastic wrap is in that drawer."

He puts the leftovers away while I finish the cleanup. Even though our activity makes noise, the silence that hung over the dining room table is still ringing in my ears and driving me batshit. I turn on the radio to cover it up. "The Moth" is on NPR and we listen to a couple of stories, sitting at the kitchen table with some coffee after everything's been put away. It's nice.

Then it's time for bed. I start to make up the sofa but he nudges me out of the way.

"I can do it."

"Well, but last night..."

"I can do it."

I go into my bedroom and close the door while I change into my pajamas. When they're on, I open it again. Jeremy looks up from his book.

"Would it be OK with you if I left my door open tonight?"

"Yeah, sure. That would be nice."

"OK, good night."

"Good night, Kevin."

I read for a while myself and then turn out the light, but I'm not sleepy. Jeremy has turned out the lights in the living room, too, but maybe he's not asleep yet.

"Jeremy?"

There's a rustle from the sofa.

"Jeremy?"

"Yeah?"

"Do you want to come into bed with me?"

He doesn't answer for a while, which confuses me.

"Are you sure?" he says at last.

"Yes."

I hear him get up from the sofa and do something with the sheet.

"Wear your night shirt."

"Oh."

I can tell he's putting it back on; that must have been the sheet noise I heard.

He pads softly into the room, dragging his pillow like a little boy with a Teddy bear. I hold open the bedclothes and he crawls in next to me, plumping the pillow before lying down on his side, his face turned toward mine. His eyes glow like an animal's in the dark.

"Hi," he says.

"Hi."

He flips onto his back and rests his head on my shoulder, just like he's done so many times in the past.

"Do you realize we've never spent a whole night together?"

He nods his head up and down. His hair tickles my nose.

"We always had to get back to our rooms. This will be a new experience."

"Better than having you sleep on the floor."

"Much better."

We shift our bodies again, snuggling even closer.

"Before you showed up last night we hadn't seen each other since your first Mass."

"I'm well aware of that."

"Well, I never thought I'd get to tell you this, but I had a pretty weird experience that day."

"I know. I saw you."

"What? What are you talking about?"

"I saw you standing with me at the altar."

"*Shit*. And I thought I just had an overactive imagination. Did you...feel me inside of you?"

Even in the dark I can sense Jeremy furrowing his brow.

"What are *you* talking about?"

"Never mind."

"I hope you don't mean what I think you mean."

"What? No, of course not. It was just...I felt like we'd become one person up there."

Jeremy is quiet for a long time after this.

"Maybe we are. Maybe that's why I couldn't make it in the parish. I was missing half of my life."

I don't say anything else, because tears have filled my eyes and I don't trust the sound of my voice. In a couple of minutes I can hear Jeremy snoring softly, and soon I'm off to sleep, too.

When I wake up I'm alone in the bed. I lie there looking at the ceiling, wondering where Jeremy's gone. Maybe he's making us breakfast, one that's up to his spoiled priestly standards. After the dinner he made last night, I can hardly wait.

I hear a muffled voice coming from the other room and realize the bedroom door has been closed. Jeremy must have the TV on.

I put on my robe and open the door and see Jeremy standing at the dining room table with his back to me. He's wearing his cassock and collar again. As I walk toward him I can see that he's set up a makeshift altar. The candles from our dinner last night are now flanking a place mat set directly in front of him. Sitting on the mat are a half-full glass of last night's shiraz and a Saltine on a saucer. Jeremy is saying Mass.

"*Unde et memores, Domine, nos servi tui, sed et plebs tua sancta, ejusdem Christi Filii tui Domini nostri...*"

His voice is weak, quavering, like he's been crying.

"*...tam beatae Passionis, nec non et ab inferis Resurrectionis, sed et in coelos gloriosae Ascensionis...*"

His hands, raised in prayer, are trembling, and his voice catches after every couple of words.

"*...offerimus praeclarae majestati tuae...de tuis donis acdatis...hostiam puram, hostiam sanctam...hostiam immaculatam.*"

He makes the sign of the cross three times over the wine and cracker, and then falls to his knees, sobbing. I rush to his side.

"*This* is what I'm supposed to *do*, Kevin. *This* is what I'm supposed to *be*. Oh God, oh God, oh *God*. Who the hell am I? What am I? I don't even know anymore."

I put my arm around his heaving shoulders, but he doesn't seem to notice.

"Oh, Jeremy, sweetheart! It'll be OK. We'll figure it out, somehow." I can't hold myself back anymore. I stroke his hair and kiss his cheek, desperate to connect with him. It doesn't work. "Do you want to try again? I could be your acolyte. I remember how."

He is still now, his arms hanging at his sides. "No." He sniffs. "It's just a stupid cracker."

His body stiffens and I can tell he wants me to let go of him, so I do.

I stand up. For a moment I have no words. "Look, I'm so sorry...I do have to get to school. There's a teachers conference before classes begin, kind of a command performance. We'll talk when I get home, OK?"

He doesn't answer. His sadness breaks my heart, and I have a feeling it's going to break even more.

I shower and dress quickly, keeping an eye on Jeremy as I go in and out of the room. He's gotten up off the floor and is sitting by the living room window, his hands limp in his lap.

"I'll see you tonight, OK?"

He doesn't even look up.

I close the front door quietly behind me, trying not to disturb him any further. I know when I get home from school he won't be here.

+   +   +

It's been three weeks since Jeremy left without saying a word. Well, he left a note, so I suppose that counts as a word, but all it said was "I'm sorry."

I stare at that scrap of paper every morning and evening, hoping to understand what, precisely, he was sorry about. Was it that he couldn't really leave the priesthood after all? Or was it that he didn't love me as much as he'd thought? I make myself crazy trying to figure out whether it's a or b, both or neither.

I'd like to believe that I can recapture the life I had before Jeremy returned to me, but it seems unlikely. I've started crying myself to sleep again, and drinking too much as well. His brief visit turned the world I'd made upside down, contaminated it with memories of him. Before Jeremy showed up it was just *my* bed, but now, for one night, it was *our* bed, so I feel his absence every time I lie down. The Beef Wellington is still sitting in the refrigerator, growing mold, because I can't bear to eat it and I can't bear to throw it away.

One bright spot: I've started hanging out at Gregory's, this bar where the music isn't too loud and you can actually talk to people, and I've made a group of friends. It's way easier to drink too much when you're having a good time, of course, but it beats the desolation I feel sitting at home, a void even John Coltrane can't fill up. The only drawback is that there's this one guy, David, who's decided I'm the one for him and won't take "no" for an answer, even though "no" is all he's gotten out of me so far. I wish he'd just give up.

I usually walk home with my friend Ben because he lives just a couple of blocks from me. Tonight we're about thirty yards from my building, comparing notes on the evening and who we think will go home with who, when I see someone sitting on my front step. I stop in my tracks.

Fuck, he's back.

Jeremy sees me, too, and perks up, like a hunting dog scenting the wind. My heart begins to pound and I start hyperventilating. Ben puts a hand on my shoulder.

"Whoa! Easy there. Trouble?"

"Like you wouldn't believe."

I bend over and put my hands on my thighs, trying to get my breath under control.

"Kevin, I've never seen you like this. Should I stick around?"

I take a few more slow, deep breaths and straighten up.

"Thanks, Ben. I'd better handle this on my own. Pray for me, will you?" Oh, and check the news tomorrow for a murder-suicide report.

I give him a peck on the cheek and he continues slowly down the street, looking back from time to time to be sure I'm OK.

I'm not OK. The only thing worse than missing Jeremy is having him show up.

I start trotting toward the building and then break into a run. I figure we might as well get this over with. Something about my energy wipes the smile off Jeremy's face and he takes two steps backward.

"Kevin, don't hit me again!"

I feel like I'm going to throw up but I manage to scream at him anyway.

"We can't keep doing this, Jeremy! We *can't*! How many times do you want to do this? How many times?" I'm putting on quite a show for the neighbors again but I'm past caring. I fall to my knees on the cold pavement, my voice hoarse with phlegm. "It's not *fair*, it's just *not fair*! You were in my bed, and the next thing I knew you were gone again, and you have *completely* fucked with my brain. So if you're back you have to be back *for good*. Otherwise just get the hell out of my life right now!"

I'm out of words. Jeremy pulls me to my feet and wraps his arms around me. I put my face on his shoulder and sob.

"Oh my God, Kevin, I'm so sorry. I thought you'd be glad to be rid of me, I was so fucked up."

He puts a hand on the back of my head and it feels so good I just cry harder.

"But it's OK now. I'm OK. I'm not here to mess with you. I'm here to stay."

His words shock me out of my tears. I raise my head and look into his face. He drops his hands to the small of my back and pulls me closer.

"To stay?" I wipe my face with the back of my hand. "You mean, with me?"

"Yes, of course with you. Unless that guy you were walking with..."

"Just a friend."

"You kissed him."

"On the *cheek*."

"I hate him anyway."

"Please don't. Let's go inside."

"OK."

Jeremy practically has to carry me into the building because my outburst took the stuffing out of me and my legs are all wobbly. He pushes 4 in the elevator and I manage to put my key in the door, but the night has taken on an air of unreality, fueled by alcohol and the rush of seeing Jeremy once again.

"Do you think you should maybe have some coffee?" he asks.

"No, I'm good. Maybe some ice water."

"I'll get it."

Oh, that's right. Jeremy knows his way around my apartment. I want to rally my senses, prepare myself for a stern conversation, but I am putty in this man's hands. I hope he'll be gentle.

As though reading my thoughts, he hands me the glass of water with the same radiant smile he gave me at his first Mass. Now at least I'm happy putty. He sits down next to me on the sofa.

"All right," I say, after a couple sips of the water. "Where have you been for the past three weeks?

"Yes, right. OK."

He seems to be organizing his thoughts. I hope they don't include anything about supplied jurisdiction this time.

"I probably freaked you out, saying Mass over a Saltine. I was so...wrapped up in my head. I couldn't even...begin to think about what it looked like for you."

"I should have stayed with you."

"It wouldn't have made any difference. I was an addict in withdrawal. You couldn't have helped."

Is there something Jeremy hasn't been telling me? "I don't get it. What's your addiction?"

He looks surprised by my question. "The Mass, Kevin, the Mass. I've been mainlining it since we were seven, and I've never been able to get enough of it. But I always had you, too. You and the Mass. Then all of a sudden I just had the Mass. I realized I had to choose. I'm sorry it took me so long."

"After you left for school, I packed up my stuff and wandered around the streets for a while. I didn't have a plan. I ended up down at the water. I...pretty seriously considered throwing myself into Puget Sound. But I...I didn't have any pants on. I didn't want my body found with my cassock over my head or something...way too undignified."

"Don't even joke about that, Jeremy."

"Um, not joking. That's what I actually thought. I decided against the whole mortal sin thing, though..."

"I'm very thankful..."

"Okay, you're welcome. So instead I got on a bus to Portland."

"You went home?"

"Yep, went to see ol' Mom and Dad."

"Wow. I just assumed you went back to the priory."

"Nope. Anyway, I was in for some surprises."

"Like what?"

"My parents have joined a *Novus Ordo* parish. They've been too embarrassed to tell me.'"

"No shit!"

"Yeah! They really like Pope Francis. They got tired of hearing him dissed from the pulpit every week. And get this: my mom tells me she always knew about me. She was hoping I'd figure it out before I did myself any harm."

"Harm?"

"I guess she was afraid I'd, like, castrate myself or something if I stuck with the Fraternity."

"Wow, that's some mother you've got."

"I know. So then I told her about you. And she said 'Oh, Kevin's such a nice boy. Tell him "hello" for me.'"

"Holy *shit*." I can't suppress a giggle at this flow of good news.

"I did go back to the rector, after that conversation. I told him I love you and want to spend the rest of my life with you."

"Um, you haven't told *me* that yet."

"I love you and I want to spend the rest of my life with you."

He moves his head in front of mine and plants a long, slow kiss on my lips.

"You should have...I don't know, *called*, or something."

"I...there's a lot I need to work on." He kisses me a second time

I place my fingertips gently on either side of his head, just to reassure myself that this is actually happening. When he sits back again I realize I'm still not clear about one thing.

"But...what about your priesthood?"

"I've started the renunciation process. Do you want to see my letter?" He sounds oddly chipper.

"No, that's OK. I'll take your word for it."

I don't want to say this, but I have to. "Are you *sure*, Jeremy? You wanted it for so long."

He smiles sweetly at me once again. "I've wanted you much longer."

We look at one another for a while in very comfortable silence. Then I know exactly what needs to come next.

"Get into that bedroom *now* and take off all your clothes."

"Why?"

"Because I need to inspect every inch of you to be sure you're all there...and all *here*. And that everything still works, of course."

"Um...OK."

As it turns out, everything is there—here—and everything works. Bliss.

+   +   +

After a late breakfast the next morning I inform Jeremy that we're going shopping.

"*Shopping?* Why?"

"To swap out those priest clothes for something a little more contemporary."

Jeremy looks down at his outfit.

"What's wrong with what I'm wearing?"

"Trust me on this. You'll be happy."

We hop on a bus to downtown and Pacific Place mall. I point out the sights along the way and rehearse the activities we'll do at each place. You know, like, during the rest of our lives. No rush. Jeremy puts his hand on top of mine as he leans across me to look out the window. I find the nearness of his face mightily distracting but keep up my tour guide patter.

The mall is huge, crowded and noisy, and Jeremy gets a deer-in-the-headlights expression on his face as soon as we pass through the revolving doors. It's not like he's been off in a mountaintop monastery, but he hasn't had any reason to go shopping for a long time, either.

"Let's make this easy," I volunteer. "The Gap is right here."

We push our way through the crowd and enter the brightly lit store.

"Welcome to The Gap, boys," says the greeter, a fey teen wearing impossibly tight jeans. "You two are darling together."

I smile politely but Jeremy purses his lips and pretends he didn't hear.

"What're you looking for today?" the greeter continues.

"Oh, pretty much everything,"

"Well," he says, waving a skinny arm toward the store's interior, "There it is!"

Much to Jeremy's relief, he's already tired of us, and turns his attention to the next customer.

"Okay, order of march. We're going to get you some jeans, some shirts, and a couple of sweaters, maybe a hoodie. Men's is on this side of the store."

The jeans display seems to reach for a city block, from floor to ceiling. The options are overwhelming. We make our way slowly between tables piled with merchandise.

"Hi, I'm Kevin and I'll be your personal shopper today," I say, doing my best impression of the greeter. Jeremy laughs in spite of himself.

"You look like you'd have a—what, 32-inch waist? And what might your inseam be?"

I look both ways and then slip my hand between Jeremy's thighs and run it down his leg.

"Kevin!" he squawks, trying to sound outraged but not really succeeding.

"Right, that feels like a 32 as well. I'll gather up some jeans for you to try on. You look at the hoodies. I'll meet you there."

I pile my arms with a selection of styles, bearing in mind that Jeremy's probably going to choose the most conservative of the bunch. When I return to him he's sorting through the hoodies like a professional, laying the ones he likes on top of the rack and quickly shunting aside the rejects.

"I forgot to ask, what are you doing for money? Do you want me to put this stuff on plastic?"

He continues to work his way through the rack, sliding the hoodies from left to right.

"Mom put some money in a checking account for me...you know, to tide me over."

"Really? How much?"

Jeremy looks at me like he doesn't get my question, then resumes his search. "Twenty thousand dollars."

"All righty, then! I guess you can get two pairs."

Jeremy drapes the hoodies he likes over one arm and we head to shirts. On the way we pass a mannequin dressed in extremely tight jeans with strategic rips all over them. Jeremy flips the tag over and reads the model name.

"'Destructed Resolution.' Get me these in my size, will you?"

"Uh, Jeremy, do you think that's a good idea?"

He looks at me blankly. "Yes."

"Okay! I'll bring them to the dressing room."

The jeans come in three shades so I get him one of each, still perplexed by his choice.

"Here you go," I say, handing them over the top of the dressing room door.

"Thanks."

I find a chair outside the dressing room and check my messages. There's one from Ben. *UOK?* What a sweetie. I text him back. *AOK. CU @ Gregory's 2nite.*

A couple more from school, an email offering a cure for my erectile dysfunction ("HA!" I say to myself as I delete it) and a goofy cat video from my cousin. I wish she would stop sending these, but I look at it anyway.

"What do you think?"

Jeremy is standing in front of me in his new outfit. He lets me look at him for a minute, then goes to find a mirror. The jeans look disconcertingly good on him, hugging him like a second skin. I'm suddenly not so sure about this. I mean, I know what he's shaped like, but I'm not sure I want everyone else to know, too. *Geez!* He's picked a gray-striped button-down shirt and the funkiest of the hoodies, also gray. He looks amazing. I'm apparently not the only one who thinks so.

"Done any modeling?"

Jeremy and I look in the mirror at the middle-aged man who's come up from behind us.

"Um, no...no, I haven't," says Jeremy.

"Here's my card," he says, as Jeremy turns to face him. "Always looking for new talent."

"Thanks," Jeremy says.

The man gives us a thin-lipped smile and walks away.

"That was cool," Jeremy says, taking another look at himself in the mirror.

"Give me that," I say, snatching the card out of his hand. *Forest Modeling Services: Your Wish Is Our Command.* I rip the card in pieces and throw it in a nearby wastebasket.

"Hey!" says Jeremy, sounding hurt. "I wanted that."

I put a hand on his sleeve.

"Jeremy, 'modeling' is just a euphemism at a place like that."

"Euphemism? For what?"

I lean in toward him, my expression earnest, waiting for the penny to drop.

"Oh."

We leave the store with all three of the Destructed Resolution jeans and an assortment of shirts and sweaters. Jeremy keeps his new outfit on and gets some high tops to replace the loafers. I struggle to keep my hands off him, he's so beautiful.

We eat a late lunch at the mall and I propose that he come to Gregory's with me tonight.

"A bar? Why? We're already together."

"Because I want you to meet my friends and have them meet you."

"Well, OK." He sounds less than enthusiastic.

"But, Jeremy?

"Yes?"

"Could you maybe put your old clothes back on before we go? I'd like to be sure you come home with me."

"We'll see," he says, leaving me to agonize.

+   +   +

I finally get to make Jeremy dinner, and I outdo myself with Chicken Kiev and an arugula salad. He's met his match in more ways than one, I guess. And so have I.

We head out to Gregory's around ten.

"Thanks for doing this. I love every minute with you but it's good to expand our circle, too. Be among our own kind."

"And this will be different from seminary how?"

"Jeremy!" I give him a little shove on his shoulder, forcing him to face me. "Did you just make a *joke*?"

"Maybe."

"Who *are* you?"

I push him back against the nearest wall and kiss him hard. He's got no force field around him anymore. He kisses me back just as hard.

When we walk into the bar I'm relieved to see that David is not among my group of regulars. Ben looks at me anxiously, trying to suss out whether I'm really OK. I give him a thumbs up, then two of them, and he can tell by my stupid grin that I really mean it. He gives me a hug.

"Yay!"

"Thanks."

I introduce Jeremy all around and I can sense that everyone picks up on the fact that this is not a casual acquaintance, even though I've never shared our complicated history. I also catch Matt wagging his hand back and forth in the universal symbol for *hot*. Jeremy, naturally, wore his new outfit, just to torment me. And make me incredibly proud as well.

Andrew offers to buy us our first drink.

"So, Jeremy, what do you do?" he asks as the waiter leaves with the order.

"Oh," Jeremy says, his voice trailing off. We probably should have discussed what our answer would be to this question.

"He's the most incredible chef," I volunteer. "Best food I've ever eaten."

"That's great!" Matt responds. "Hoping to do that here in Seattle?"

"Why, yes," Jeremy says. "I am."

"So, tell us how you met..."

"We grew up together," I say. That's an easy one.

"Wow, cool! Then, when did you become a couple?"

"Oh," we say together. We haven't thought this through at all. We look at each other, then burst out laughing.

"This is going to be *way* too hard, Kevin. Let's just tell them."

He turns back to the group.

"We became a couple in seminary."

"Oh!" says Jonathan. "I went to seminary, too! Which one?"

"Uh, you probably haven't heard of it," I say.

"Try me. I know every Protestant seminary there is."

"It wasn't Protestant."

"Really?" Jonathan knits his brow. "You got together in a *Catholic* seminary?"

"Well," Jeremy says, "let's just call it that."

Over the next half hour we tell them the whole story, and everyone is so engrossed the waiter starts to pout because no one is drinking. "What's got you boys so hot and bothered?" he asks petulantly.

Matt hears the real message. "Sorry, just bring us all another round."

The group picks up their watery drinks as one and chug-a-lugs them, slamming the glasses down on the table in unison.

"Go on," Andrew says, breathlessly.

And we do. And it's wonderful, for us as well as for them. It feels so *liberating*. We're having a great time until David shows up.

It's clear right away that this isn't David's first bar of the evening. In fact, he seems pretty drunk. My heart sinks when I see him come through the door, but then I lose him in the crowd. Suddenly he's right behind my chair.

"Kevin," he says thickly.

I jump to my feet, not sure what to do next.

"Uh, hi, David. There's someone here I'd like you to meet. David, this is Jeremy. Jeremy, David."

David turns and looks at Jeremy but can't seem to focus. "Huh."

Jeremy extends his hand but David ignores it.

"Kevin, you're so goddam *hot*. How long you gonna make me wait for a taste of those sweet lips?"

And with that he grabs my face and kisses me, sticking his tongue into my mouth before I know what's going on. He tastes of pepperoni and cigarettes.

Even as I'm trying to get David off of me I can hear Jeremy muttering in Latin. "*Exorcizo te, immundissime spiritus, omnis incursio adversarii.*" It's the rite of exorcism, but I doubt even that is going to slow David down.

"David, please! I'm here with Jeremy. You're embarrassing yourself."

David looks at Jeremy a second time.

"Really, with *him*? The pretty boy? What's he got that I haven't got? Oh, I guess I just answered that one." He belches loudly. "Well, we'll have to do something about that..."

When they hear this everybody stands up, sensing trouble.

"David, for heaven's sake, just leave Kevin alone," Andrew says. "Go bother some other table."

David starts slamming his fist into his palm, clearly intending its next target to be Jeremy's face. I come around the table and stand in front of him, but Jeremy pushes me out of the way and looks his would-be assailant directly in the eye.

"Listen—David, is it?—there's no need for this."

"There is, though."

"Well, David, I'll have you know that I'm a priest, a Catholic priest, and I'm sure you would never hit a priest, would you?" Jeremy strokes his jaw apprehensively.

David pounds Jeremy smack on the nose. He falls backwards against my chest and my arms instinctively wrap around him in protection, except what I end up doing is holding him in place like a target so David can sock him in the gut.

"Oof! Dammit, Kevin, let go of me! You're not helping."

"Sorry, sorry!"

Jeremy is about to return David's blow when the bouncer grabs his hand. (Who knew Gregory's had a bouncer?) "Not in here, boys! Not that kind of place. Take it outside."

Violence is such a rarity here that the entire bar has gathered around us and now follows excitedly as Jeremy and David head out to the street. To my dismay, I get stuck in the press of the crowd.

"Let me through! Let me through, dammit!"

By the time I get outside, it's already over. Jeremy is down on one knee, wiping blood off his lip, but David is lying on the sidewalk in a fetal position, moaning.

"Do you think he needs an ambulance?" I ask.

Jeremy looks in David's direction. "No, but if he ever puts his grubby hands on you again he'll need a hearse."

I help Jeremy get to his feet. The crowd applauds, then starts heading back inside. Poor David. Seems no one much likes him. The bouncer, at least, has gone to offer him a cold towel.

When we're almost alone again Jeremy puts his chin in the air and looks down his nose at me in a superior way.

"I have won your hand in combat. You are mine, now. Come, wench, home to my bed, where I will have my way with you."

"Did you just call me your *wench*? Really?"

Jeremy has always made me happy but he's never made me laugh. This is the second time tonight.

"Wench?"

Now I'm the one laughing till I almost choke.

Jeremy reaches out a hand to me.

"Well, come on. *Come on.*"

Wiping a tear from my eye, I take his hand and we stroll off into the night.

+   +   +

Eight months on, and life is good. Actually, life is great. Jeremy is apprenticing with one of Seattle's best chefs, my school is sending me to get Waldorf certification, which means I can get tenure, and my parents have invited us to come for Thanksgiving. Will wonders never cease? I can pray again, and that makes me happy. Jeremy and I even pray together before meals, holding hands across the table. (Thank you, *Novus Ordo* Mass!) So it seems that nothing has been wasted, nothing at all.

Ubi caritas et amor, Deus ibi est.

Where love and charity are, there is God.

The Trials of Jody

From the moment he woke up Jody knew it was going to be a blessed day, maybe even a miraculous one. He lingered under the covers, watching the shadows of leaves flutter on the bedroom window shade and daydreaming about all the ways God had blessed his life. First and foremost, there was Brian, his sweet and incredibly hot boyfriend. Then there were his pals from church, all of whom he loved dearly, and this great apartment he'd found in West Hollywood for an unbelievably low rent, and his fun job as the digital archivist for a hip radio station. Jody had it all, and he was so grateful to God he felt he might just burst out in a doxology if he didn't have such a bad singing voice. To top it all off, today was his birthday, and Brian and all his friends were coming over later to celebrate it with him.

Jody was in such a good mood that when he finally got out of bed and stepped on a snail that had somehow gotten past the screen door during the night, smearing its black blubber all over his sole and embedding bits of its shattered shell between his toes, it didn't strike him as a bad omen.

"Sorry, little guy! Didn't mean to kill ya! Hope you enjoy Snail Heaven!"

Jody tried to picture a group of snails sitting on clouds, holding harps, but then he realized they didn't have any hands to hold them with. He shrugged.

"Oh, well, listening is good, too."

He wiped his foot with a Kleenex from the bedside table and then used it to gather up the remains of the snail. He didn't want a dead snail in his bedroom wastebasket, so he decided to take it outside to the garbage. Jody padded across the pleasantly cool floor and opened the door to the living room. Just in time, he grabbed the door frame to prevent himself from taking another step.

The entire living room floor was covered with snails.

"Holy shit!" Jody yelled, then covered his mouth and looked skyward. "Sorry, sorry, sorry!" he called out to the ceiling.

Maybe God hadn't heard that one. He probably had more to do today than worry about cuss words. Jody returned his gaze to the snails. It seemed like every snail in California had assembled in his apartment. He had no idea what to do.

Well, he had one idea. Put on some shoes.

Dressed and shod, Jody picked his way through the living room to the kitchen, trying his best to avoid the strange little creatures, but despite his best efforts, with every third or fourth step he heard a disgusting crunch sound. By the time he reached the kitchen he'd lost any appetite for breakfast.

He flipped open his laptop on the kitchen counter and Googled pest control. Orkin listed snails as one of their targets of destruction so he gave them a call.

"Can you send someone right away? I need to get to work."

"For snails? They're not exactly an emergency. How many can you see? Three, four?"

Jody surveyed his living room and gave his best estimate.

"Maybe two thousand."

"Jesus!" the Orkin representative hissed. Jody frowned.

"Wait a minute," the woman said. "Is this some kind of prank?"

"I wish it was. If you're willing to give me your cell number I'll call you right back in FaceTime and then you can see for yourself."

"Well...okay, I guess."

Jody opened FaceTime and entered the phone number the woman had given him.

"Okay, I'm going to walk out into the living room a little bit," he said, pointing his phone toward the floor.

"I'll send someone right away," the Orkin lady said.

Even if they showed up quickly Jody was going to be late for work, so he called his boss.

"Hi, Anton! You're not going to believe this, but...I've got a lot of snails in my living room."

"Snails?"

"Yeah. The exterminator is coming over, so I'll be a little late this morning."

"Take all the time you want," Anton said in a distinctly unfriendly tone that puzzled Jody.

"Is everything okay?"

"No, Jody, everything is not okay. You remember when I asked you to move all of the Dead Can Dance files to the new server?"

"Yes?"

"Do you have any idea where they are now?"

"Um...on the new server?"

"Wrong. They aren't anywhere. Not on the old server, not on the new server, nowhere. Gone. Vanished."

Jody was sure he had handled the transfer correctly. "When I get in I'll find them for you."

"Don't bother, Jody. I paid a small fortune for the broadcast rights for those files, and that money's down the toilet now. You're fired. I'll put your two weeks' pay in the mail. Barb will clean out your desk and leave everything in a box at the receptionist's counter."

Anton hung up. Jody put his phone down on the counter, speechless. Between the snails and losing his job, he was not having a very good birthday.

"Dear heavenly Father," he prayed in a gentle voice. "Please help me to be strong this day. I need your love and guidance. Please be with the hand of the Orkin man so that he can cast the snails out of my living room as Moses cast the frogs out of Egypt. And please soften the heart of Anton so he changes his mind about firing me. Amen."

As soon as he had prayed for Anton to change his mind Jody decided he could help answer that prayer by going to the office and finding those files, assuming Anton would let him in the door. He grabbed his keys off the hook on the refrigerator and opened the door to the carport.

Which was empty.

Jody's arms fell limply to his side as his mouth opened in disbelief. The keys slipped from his hand and clattered cheerfully on the concrete floor.

"What the hell is going on?" he said out loud, and this time he sent no apologies heavenward. He had just made his last car payment. The car was all his, except now it was all someone else's. This was too much. He needed Brian.

Jody took out his phone and pressed the power button. The screensaver of him and Brian at the beach popped up, offering him the first bit of comfort he'd had that day. He pressed Brian's speed dial and waited. The call went straight to voice mail.

"Hey, Brian here. You know the drill."

After the beep, Jody poured out his sad story.

"Honey, it's me. You won't believe the day I'm having. My apartment is infested with snails. And when I say infested I mean, like, thousands of them. I called Anton to say I'd be late and he fired me over the phone, because he says I lost some files that I know I did not lose. So I was going to drive to work anyway to prove the files aren't lost, and now it turns out someone has stolen my car. Can you believe that? I am so not having a blessed day. Can you please drive me to the police station so I can file a report? Please? I need to see you, baby. Help!"

The Orkin truck pulled up to the curb and Jody realized that if his car had not been stolen he would have missed his chance to get the house cleared of the snails. The exterminator did not look anything like the Abercrombie and Fitch models in Orkin's TV commercials. He was short and fat and had a pungent body odor even at this early hour of the morning.

"So, I hear you got some snails. Where are they?" the Orkin man asked, craning to see over Jody's shoulder, as though the snails might be sitting in the chairs or hanging from the ceiling.

"It's more like 'where aren't they'?" Jody said as he stood out of the way to let the man in.

Still looking for the snails at waist height, the man had smashed at least ten of them underfoot before he thought to look down at the ground. He jumped back a surprisingly long distance given his physique.

"Holy moley! How the hell did you get so many snails in here?"

"Could you watch your language, please? I don't know. I just woke up and there they were."

"Jesus Fuckin' Christ."

Jody wanted to ask the man to leave but he wanted his magic chemicals more.

"Sir? Language?"

"What?" The Orkin man looked distracted. "Oh, yeah, right. Just never seen so many goddamned snails in one place." He turned and looked Jody in the eye.

"It's gonna smell when I get done with them. I'll kill 'em and cart 'em away, but you're gonna have to get someone else to aerate the house."

Jody sighed. Nothing could surprise him any more

"Okay."

The Orkin man was efficient about killing and clearing the snails, but he was right about the odor. Jody had never smelled a rotting corpse, but this was pretty much what he imagined it would be like. He called Brian and got voice mail again.

"Baby, where are you? The snails are gone but now there's an awful smell in the house. It's making me gag. Can I stay at your place for a few days? Call me soon, okay?"

Jody handed the Orkin man a credit card, which he ran through a transponder like the rental car places use.

"So that'll be— "

"Don't tell me! I'll find out when the bill comes." Jody didn't want to think about how he would pay off the card with no income. He'd just have to find another job...fast.

"Huh? Okay, whatever you say." The Orkin man let himself out the front door and said, without a trace of irony in his voice, "Have a nice day."

Jody searched the police department's website and found that he could download the missing vehicle report but he'd still have to present it in person to verify that he was the car's owner. He found the registration information, filled out the form, and hiked to the bus stop to go downtown.

The police station was crowded, and none of the employees seemed to be in any particular hurry to rid West Hollywood of crime, so Jody ended up waiting hours to file his report. He wished he'd brought his Bible to read. And when he put his hand in his pocket, he realized with a start that he'd left his phone on the kitchen counter, so he couldn't even get Brian's call or tell him to come pick him up.

When he finally got home he raced to his phone but Brian hadn't called. He did have sixteen new texts, however. They were all from his church friends who were coming to give him a birthday party tonight.

SO SORRY. WON'T MAKE IT TONIGHT AFTER ALL. HAPPY BDAY ANYWAY.

BAD NEWS. NEED TO WORK TONIGHT. HAVE A BLAST.

MY SISTER JUST HAD HER BABY. SORRY TO MISS PARTY. SEE YOU IN CHURCH.

And so on. When he'd finally gotten through all the texts he realized there were only three people left on the guest list who hadn't declined: Michael, Perry and Carlos. He stared at the display, expecting to see three new texts pop up any moment. Had they all planned this? How could it be a coincidence?

The phone rang with Brian's ringtone, "I Want to Sex You Up."

"Finally!" Jody said, eagerly pushing Accept.

"Where have you been, baby? I've been waiting all day to hear from you."

"Uh, yeah...sorry about that."

"Well, what's up? Why haven't you called?"

"Uh...Jody, we need to talk."

"Jesus Fuckin' Christ!" Jody practically yelled into the phone. "Are you breaking up with me on my birthday, asshole?" Jody could practically feel Brian's shock on the other end. Up until now, he'd have apologized if 'darn' popped out of his mouth.

"I've never heard you talk like that," Brian said at last.

"I've never had a day like this. So is that what we need to talk about? Our break-up?"

"Uh, more or less."

"Over the phone and on my birthday. Can I pick 'em or what?"

Brian was silent.

"It's Robert, isn't it?

More silence.

"I knew I never should have let you two go to Comic-Con with each other. I could tell he had his eye on you."

"It wasn't like that."

"Yeah? Well I don't care what it was like. This is the worst birthday of my whole goddamned life."

He pushed End Call with as much vehemence as he could muster. He regretted not having a chance to slam a mouthpiece down on a receiver the way he'd seen in old movies.

He totted up the day's casualties: He now had no car, no boyfriend, no birthday party, and a stinky house. He threw open the door of the nearly-empty refrigerator and fished out the carton of leftover Kung Pao chicken. He used a spoon to skim off the fuzzy bits and went into the living room to watch TV while he ate his dinner cold out of the carton, making his misery complete.

Two hours later he was able to take a break from vomiting just long enough to call an ambulance. Sitting in the ER after they'd pumped his stomach he looked glumly at his phone, wondering if his three remaining friends had bailed on him as well. There was a voice mail from Carlos.

"Hey, birthday boy, where are you? Perry and Michael and I are at your house with cake and wine but you're not here. Hope everything's okay. Call me and tell me what's up."

With tears of gratitude filling his eyes, Jody pressed Return Call.

"There you are, *bicho*!" Carlos said brightly. "Did we get the wrong night?"

"No, no, it's my birthday. But I'm in the Emergency Room."

"Whaaa?" Carlos said, sounding like Ricky Ricardo.

"Yeah, I ate something bad and it gave me food poisoning. They just pumped my stomach out."

"Is Brian with you?"

"Um, no."

"Well, don't go anywhere! We'll be right over to get you and take you home."

"Don't worry," Jody said, but Carlos had already hung up.

Forty-five minutes later they walked into Jody's apartment.

"What on earth is that smell?" Perry asked, crinkling his nose.

"Snail poison," Jody said dispiritedly. The morning now seemed a lifetime ago.

"Well, let's at least open some windows," said Michael. "Phew!"

"Have you got a fan?" Carlos asked.

"In the closet."

Jody was still wearing the clothes he'd vomited in, so he went to his bedroom to change and freshen up. When he came out in a white terry bath robe the fan was roaring on High and his friends were waving towels and a kitchen rug to air out the room. It looked like some kind of bizarre gay Rite of Spring, but it was actually reducing the odor.

"I'm sorry I can't help, guys, but I'm just all tuckered out." Jody collapsed into an armchair.

"Don't even think about helping," Michael said. "You want some tea?"

"Yeah, that would be great. Cabinet next to the stove."

Michael fixed Jody's tea while the others got themselves plates of cake and glasses of wine, sitting at a discreet distance from the birthday boy so the smells didn't make his stomach churn.

"Where's Brian?" asked Perry cheerfully, failing to see Carlos's "zip it" gesture in time. Carlos had already figured out that if Brian hadn't been at the hospital, there had to be a problem.

"Brian? He gone," said Jody lazily, lolling his head on the back of the armchair.

"Gone? Like to the store?" Perry was not the sharpest knife in the drawer.

"Gone, like out of my life. He broke up with me this evening. Over the phone. On my birthday."

Sympathetic murmurs ran through the trio.

"It was Robert, wasn't it?" asked Carlos.

"Did everyone know but me?"

"That little..."

"Language!" reminded Michael primly.

"*Pichoncito*, I'm so sorry. You didn't deserve this, especially not on your birthday. The snails, the break-up, going to the hospital, it's all terrible."

"My car was stolen, too," Jody said bitterly.

"Whaaaa?" Carlos asked a second time.

"And you were the only three who didn't bail on my birthday party. I guess I know who my friends are, now."

Michael had a look of concentration on his face.

"Can these bad things all be just coincidences?"

Everyone turned and looked at him.

"What else would they be?"

"Well, he must have done something to deserve all these, what shall we call them, 'calamities.'"

"Michael, what are you suggesting?"

"Nobody just wakes up to two thousand snails in their living room. God must be sending Jody a message."

"Like what? Jody's a big sweetheart. What could he possibly have done to make God mad at him?"

Michael absently scratched the back of his head and looked at the floor. "Well, there's that thing in Leviticus. 'Thou shalt not lie with a man as with a woman...'"

"What? You think God is punishing Jody for being gay?" Carlos was apoplectic. "Michael, you lie with men as with a woman, and you've probably done it hundreds of times! God doesn't seem to be punishing you."

Michael sniffed. "Just sayin'..."

Perry jumped on Michael's bandwagon.

"Maybe Michael has a point."

All heads now whipped in Perry's direction.

"Those snails sound like one of the plagues of Egypt," he went on. "Not natural. No good explanation..."

"And your point is?" asked Carlos irritably.

"I'm not sure yet. Jody, can you think of a reason God would be mad at you? Have you been taking office supplies from the studio? Jerking off—I mean, masturbating—more than usual? Pastor Kevin says it's not a sin in itself but it can be when it becomes...excessive."

"Really? How many times is excessive?"

Michael looked anxious.

"He didn't say," Perry answered, offhandedly.

"Well, is it, like, more than three times a day?"

"Michael! Too much information!"

Michael clamped his mouth shut, still looking worried.

Perry persisted. "What about it, Jody? Can you think of something *else* you've done to offend God?"

"*Nooo!*" Jody replied crossly. "I read my Bible. I go to church. I pray! Morning, noon and night. And I am strictly monogamous. Well, I guess technically I haven't been recently, but I didn't know about Robert so it doesn't count."

Jody realized that along with his boyfriend and his car he had lost his faith today.

"Well...if God can punish someone like me, then He doesn't deserve my love or my praise. In fact, as far as I'm concerned, God can just go fuck himself."

Jody's friends looked at him in horror, their mouths hanging open in stereotypical expressions of disbelief. He stared back at them defiantly, waiting for someone to speak, but they were silent. Silent and unmoving. Someone or something had frozen them in time.

Jody looked down at his own hands, to see if he was frozen, too, but no, he had normal movement. What was going on?

A small dot of violet appeared on the widescreen TV, even though he hadn't turned it on. As Jody watched, the dot grew, and began to seethe like boiling lava or a stop-motion movie of a flower bursting into bloom played at high speed.

Other gem tones joined the violet, and soon the entire screen was awash in vibrant, textured, moving colors.

"SO I CAN GO FUCK MYSELF, CAN I?"

The powerful voice came from the direction of the TV but seemed to fill the whole room. Jody gulped. The voice continued.

"PUT OFF THY SHOES FROM OFF THY FEET..."

Jody glanced at his bare feet propped up on the ottoman.

"FOR THE PLACE WHEREON THOU STANDEST IS HOLY GROUND...."

Jody had seen *The Ten Commandments* multiple times. If this was really God speaking to him, He got low marks for originality.

"First of all, I'm not wearing any shoes. Second of all, this holy ground happens to be my apartment. And I don't recall inviting you!"

"FIRST OF ALL," the voice replied, sounding peeved. "ANY PLACE I SHOW UP IS HOLY GROUND. AND SECOND OF ALL..."

The voice paused.

"WELL, I DON'T ACTUALLY HAVE A SECOND OF ALL. BUT I CANNOT BE TOLD TO GO FUCK MYSELF WITHOUT MANIFESTING MYSELF TO SET MY CALUMNIATOR STRAIGHT. SO TO SPEAK."

The voice was impressive but hard to define. Was it male? Female? White? Black? Asian? Jody wasn't sure.

"'Calumniator'? Is that a thing?"

"YES, IT'S A THING."

"Well, I've never heard of it."

"LET ME GOOGLE THAT FOR YOU."

"All right, all right. Spare me the sarcasm. Geez, who knew God was a bitter old queen?" Jody thought he had said the last thing to himself but apparently he hadn't.

"SILENCE!" roared the voice, making Jody cower a bit in spite of himself. "I AM NEITHER A BITTER OLD QUEEN NOR AN ANGRY BLACK WOMAN NOR A SERENE BUDDHA-LIKE FIGURE OF INDETERMINATE GENDER, BUT AN INEFFABLE COMBINATION OF ALL OF THESE. I AM WHAT I AM..."

"'And what I am needs no excuses...' Give me a break."

"OH, YOU'VE SEEN THAT MOVIE? I THOUGHT YOU'D BE TOO YOUNG."

"Yeah, we had to watch it for my Gay Cultural History class."

The voice was silent, apparently fresh out of conversational gambits. Jody decided to take the lead.

"Did you send the snails?"

"YES."

"Why?"

"BECAUSE I CAN."

"No, really."

"TO GET YOUR ATTENTION."

"Well, you've got it now. Everything else today, is that you, too?"

"NO. I DIDN'T SEE ROBERT COMING, EITHER. BUT IT GOT THE RIGHT RESULT."

"Namely, to ruin my birthday?"

"MORE OR LESS."

"Why would you want to do that?"

"BECAUSE YOUR HAPPINESS WAS BASED ON ALL THE GOOD THINGS IN YOUR LIFE AND NOT ROOTED IN YOUR HEART. I WANTED TO SEE WHAT WOULD HAPPEN IF ALL THOSE GOOD THINGS WERE TAKEN AWAY."

"Well I saw! It crushed my spirit."

"DID IT? YOU'VE GOT ENOUGH SPIRIT TO ARGUE WITH GOD."

Jody considered this.

"YOU GAVE BRIAN A PIECE OF YOUR MIND INSTEAD OF BURSTING INTO TEARS, AND YOU WERE VERY ORGANIZED ABOUT FILING THE POLICE REPORT AND GETTING RID OF THE SNAILS. INSTEAD OF BEING DEFEATED WHEN ANTON FIRED YOU, YOU FORMED A PLAN TO GET YOUR JOB BACK. I THINK YOU'VE LEARNED HOW STRONG YOU REALLY ARE TODAY."

Jody pulled his legs off the ottoman and sat forward in the chair.

"You know, you're kind of right."

The throbbing colors on the TV screen grew a bit brighter.

"KIND OF RIGHT...GREAT."

Jody stood up and started pacing around the room. It felt weird to walk in and out of his silent friends, who looked like department store mannequins. He picked up the birthday cake from the plate Perry was holding in midair and crammed it into this mouth.

"Mmmffy nobday fafferall..." he said.

"NOT GETTING THAT."

Jody swallowed the cake and took a swig of Michael's wine.

"I said, 'Maybe this isn't such a bad birthday after all. Maybe I did let my happiness depend too much on other people, or all the right circumstances. It was a terrible day, but I survived it."

"YOU DID," said the voice, with a distinct note of approval.

"Wow, I never really put it together. All those people I learned about in that gay history class, they went through a lot worse than I did today. They were beaten, and put in jail, and fired from their jobs—for being gay, I mean, not because their boss was an asshole—and sometimes they lost their family and friends. But they kept going."

"THAT'S RIGHT, JODY. YOU HAVE A LOT YOU HAVE TAKEN FOR GRANTED. YOU HAVE GAY MARRIAGE NOW! (AND, BY THE WAY, I DID THAT.) BUT IF THAT GUY WITH THE YELLOW HAIR BECOMES PRESIDENT YOU MAY NEED A LITTLE PERSEVERENCE."

"He doesn't care about gays."

"I KNOW THAT. I'M OMNISCIENT."

"You didn't see Robert coming."

"I WILL IGNORE THAT. ALL I KNOW IS HE CARES ABOUT GETTING VOTES FROM PEOPLE WHO CARE BOUT GAYS, AND NOT IN A GOOD WAY."

"If you're really omniscient, who's going to win?"

"I CAN READ MANY DIFFERENT FUTURES. BUT THEY ALL DEPEND ON YOU. WITH THAT FREE WILL OF YOURS, WHO KNOWS WHAT YOU'LL DO NEXT? DON'T JUST CONCENTRATE ON ALL THE GOOD THINGS YOU'VE GOT. MAKE THE WORLD A BETTER PLACE WHILE YOU'RE IN IT."

"A better place..." Jody murmured. "Isn't that your job? We're always praying for you to end wars and cure sick people."

"YEAH, HOW'S THAT WORKING OUT FOR YOU?"

Jody smiled ruefully.

"You're really not much like the God I've been praying to all my life."

"NO, I'M NOT."

"So you think I can, like, actually make a difference?"

"I KNOW YOU CAN. YOU'RE A GOOD KID."

"Thanks!"

Jody suddenly felt like crying.

"AND LET'S NOT FORGET THAT GREAT ASS I GAVE YOU AS A BONUS."

Jody blushed. He never thought he would be discussing his ass, which was, admittedly, perfect, with the Creator of the Universe.

"I owe you one for that," he said shyly.

"DON'T MENTION IT. WE MAY NOT SPEAK LIKE THIS AGAIN, JODY. IT'S MORE OR LESS A ONE-OFF. BUT I'LL BE THERE, CHEERING YOU ON, WANTING THE BEST FOR YOU. REMEMBER, IT'S ALL ABOUT LOVE AND JUSTICE."

"Love and justice," Jody repeated. "I'll remember."

The swirling colors on the TV screen collapsed back into themselves until only the single dot of violet remained, then that disappeared, too.

"Jody, I'm sure you didn't mean that," Perry said. "Hey, where's my cake?"

"You're right, Perry, I didn't. It's just been a really bad day. But I think I'm going to be OK now."

The friends looked at each other and smiled, relieved that Jody had recanted his blasphemy. The doorbell began to ring over and over. Someone really wanted in.

Jody walked calmly to the front door and opened it. He knew what would be on the other side. All the friends who had blown off his birthday party had now shown up, bearing food and gifts and balloons and looking sheepish. They began to make their apologies all at once, drowning each other out. Anton was behind them, joining the chorus, saying the files were on the new server after all, and would Jody please come back to work on Monday? Brian was on one knee in front of the whole group, wearing his best hangdog expression and holding up an engagement ring in a black box. Jody turned his head to look into the carport, and, sure enough, there sat his car, the word "SORRY" written with a finger in the dust on the hood.

Jody looked over the smiling, pleading, faces, saying nothing. They'd all let him down, every one of them.

He turned and looked back into the living room at the silent blackness of the TV screen. The words echoed in his brain: "Remember, it's all about love and justice." He decided he'd start with love and work his way up to justice. He pulled the front door fully back and stood aside.

"Come in," he said. "Come in, all of you."

ABOUT THE AUTHOR

John Addison Dally grew up in a non-religious family in the suburbs of Chicago. When he became a Christian at 17 and then an Episcopal priest in his early twenties they shook their heads, but gave him a nice waffle iron as an ordination gift. His shockingly queer Ph.D. dissertation won the Marc Perry Galler prize at the University of Chicago, a turn of events he attributes to a bureaucratic mix-up, but he's not giving the money back. He has been married to his husband for 34 years, 13 of them legally.

ABOUT TORTOISE BOOKS

Slow and steady wins in the end, even in publishing. Tortoise Books is dedicated to finding and promoting quality authors who haven't yet found a niche in the marketplace—writers producing memorable and engaging works that will stand the test of time.

Learn more at www.tortoisebooks.com, find us on Facebook, or follow us on Twitter @TortoiseBooks.

CPSIA information can be obtained
at www.ICGtesting.com
Printed in the USA
LVHW050741141021
700269LV00003BA/7